VINDICATED BY A VISCOUNT

The Beresford Adventures
Book 5

Cheryl Bolen

ARE YOU SIGNED UP FOR DRAGONBLADE'S BLOG?

You'll get the latest news and information on exclusive giveaways, exclusive excerpts, coming releases, sales, free books, cover reveals and more.

Check out our complete list of authors, too!

No spam, no junk. That's a promise!

Sign Up Here

www.dragonbladepublishing.com

Dearest Reader;

Thank you for your support of a small press. At Dragonblade Publishing, we strive to bring you the highest quality Historical Romance from some of the best authors in the business. Without your support, there is no 'us', so we sincerely hope you adore these stories and find some new favorite authors along the way.

Happy Reading!

CEO, Dragonblade Publishing

Additional Dragonblade books by Author Cheryl Bolen

The Beresford Adventures
Lady Mary's Dangerous Encounter (Book 1)
My Lord Protector (Book 2)
With a Little Help from My Lord (Book 3)
Rescued by a Rake (Book 4)
Vindicated by a Viscount (Book 5)

CHAPTER ONE

E VEN THOUGH MISS Georgiana Beresford knew that her sister,
Lucy, would have apoplexy, Georgiana was determined to
dash over to their cousin Harriett's house. *Without a chaperone.*
After all, the journey would take less than two minutes. A nasty
cold prevented Lucy from chaperoning her younger sister, and
Georgiana did not wish to inconvenience her maid by demanding
her presence on so short a walk.

That poor servant was being tasked with washing, ironing,
and mending Georgiana's dress that had met with an unfortunate
episode the previous evening. It really hadn't been Georgiana's
fault. Harriett's cat had a lamentable habit of hiding himself
beneath Georgiana's skirts without her knowledge. Consequently, when Georgiana began to leave her cousin's chamber, she
stumbled over the cat and ended up sitting in a lusty dog's dinner
bowl.

In spite of being a pet lover herself, Georgiana concurred with
the rest of the Beresfords: Harriett was in possession of too many
pets.

"If Lady Montague asks for me, I've gone to Lady Rockingham's," Georgiana told Peg, who was in the process of warming
an iron.

Peg looked up from bending over the hearth, squinting
through pale lashes. "By yerself, miss?"

"Yes. I doubt it's even a two-minute walk."

"True, but yer sister won't be 'appy about you traipsing around London alone."

"I fail to see why it's permissible for you to go hither and yon alone, but I cannot."

"I'm not Quality like you, miss. The men in yer class won't marry a soiled lady. Gots to be sure their heirs be from their own seed."

Oh, dear. Georgiana hadn't expected such a blunt explanation. Peg might be just two years older than her mistress, but in so many ways, she was much wiser.

"My family can be assured I will do nothing to jeopardize my prospects of marrying. I'm getting dangerously close to being glued to the shelf."

"No, yer not! Twenty's not so old, and yer awfully pretty. Yer just too particular."

Georgiana shrugged. "I truly do want to marry." She slipped on her spencer, tied on the bonnet that most closely matched it, and proceeded to leave the house. She was still trying to get used to her sister being married to Lord Montague and living in one of the finest mansions on London's Piccadilly Street.

As soon as she stepped foot on the crowded pavement, she regretted not having donned something warmer than a spencer. The air was cold enough to frost windows and still damp from last night's rain.

Georgiana passed Lord Burlington's house as well as that of his kinsman, the Duke of Devonshire. A variety of shops catering to the wealthy mingled among the sprawling mansions of the aristocracy. She eyed a fine milliner's and vowed to go there when Lucy was feeling better. The slender shop next to it sold London's finest gloves and was patronized by an exclusive clientele.

A woman leaving the glovemaker's caught Georgiana's eyes. She was dressed beautifully in an exquisite lavender gown with a woolen pelisse of the same color and an elaborate hat from which a lavender ostrich feather jutted smartly. Georgiana was so taken with the woman's clothing she hadn't actually looked at the woman who displayed such uncommonly good taste.

The many pedestrians swarming the pavement prevented Lucy from getting a good look at the lovely creature. Then, when a pair of elderly women shuffled farther away, Lucy managed to see the woman's profile. She was extraordinarily beautiful. In fact, she bore a strong resemblance to a woman Lucy once knew. Her hair was black, like the other woman. And her figure was perfection. Like the other woman. Both women were even the same average height.

Georgiana wasn't close enough to see her eyes. The other woman, a Mrs. Powell, was possessed of extraordinary blue eyes, much like Lucy's. Everyone said they were Lucy's best feature.

The Beauty approached a fine carriage. Just before she stepped in, her head turned, and their eyes locked. Georgiana's heartbeat exploded. This could not be the humble Mrs. Powell Lucy had known, but she looked exactly like her! This stunning woman's eyes were the color of the sky on a cloudless summer day. The same as Mrs. Powell's.

The woman quickly looked away and hurried into the coach that bore a shiny gold crest of the nobility. Georgiana rushed to the coach as it pulled away. Her shoe slipped on the wet pavement, and she went flying onto the puddled street, landing like a squished bird splayed on a window.

Pain seared from ankle to hip, and her gloved hands, now muddy, stung. She was quite sure something dreadful had happened to her right thigh. Or hip. She couldn't tell because the radiating pain was so intense.

Before she could attempt to put weight on her leg, someone was lifting her. She found herself enclosed in a pair of strong arms. Her gaze climbed to see who was attached to those arms. She was mortified to discover she'd been assisted by an exceedingly handsome young man.

She could not have looked worse. Not only were her previously white gloves now soaked brown, but a mixture of tea-colored water and mud stained her pink dress and saturated her hair.

"That was a beastly fall," he said in a cultured voice. Everything about his perfect face conveyed earnestness as he looked down at her with honeyed brown eyes the same color as his stylishly cut hair.

She was aware that she probably was not able to walk. "Indeed."

"You must be in great pain."

She hated to admit the extent of her pain. It was bad enough that her unladylike mishap had been observed. She responded with a half-hearted shrug.

"Where can I take you?"

Her sister's home, where she'd been staying, was still closer than her cousin's house on Half Moon Street. "Just a few houses back. At Montague House."

His face went even more somber. "Are you the new Lady Montague?"

"No. That's my sister. I'm staying with her."

As they strode along the pavement, onlookers gawked. She wished she could sink her face into his chest. What a sight she must be! Even if she hadn't looked so bedraggled, being carried along a London Street by such a well-dressed gentleman could never have gone unnoticed. She couldn't meet the eyes of those who pointed at her. Or those who snickered. Most of all, she was embarrassed by the laughter that met them at each step. Thank the sweet heavens she wasn't far from Lucy's house!

In less than a minute, he was presenting them at the shiny black door of Montague House. The footman's eyes widened when he swung open the door. "Miss Beresford! Are you all right?"

The handsome man answered. "We don't know yet. Where can I take her?"

She answered in a commanding voice. "The drawing room,

please."

The footman led the way as her rescuer mounted the staircase and brought her to the drawing room.

"Pray, Thompson, could you fetch something to cover the sofa?" she asked the footman. "I shan't wish to get it dirty. You see, I've fallen and gotten quite dirty."

"Again?" Then, embarrassed over his inappropriate comment, he quietly added, "Forgive me. I'm deeply sorry for your latest . . . injury. I'm off to locate a blanket or such." He scurried from the chamber.

"I'm going to set you down now," the man told her. "We need to see if you're able to stand." He came to the blazing fire and lowered her until she stood before the hearth.

She winced.

"It hurts when you stand?" he asked.

Eyes narrowed, she frowned. "Yes, it does rather."

He surprised her by once again scooping her into his arms.

"I feel so ridiculous," she said.

"Don't."

Something about this man's commanding presence intimidated her. She wanted to protest, to insist that she did not need to be held, but she was powerless to defy him.

A moment later, a screeching Lucy hurried into the chamber. "What's happened? Thompson says you've been hurt. Again."

Thompson, carrying a length of linen sheeting, trailed his mistress into the room and began to spread it over the silken sofa.

Why did everyone keep stressing her propensity to meet with unfortunate accidents? She was embarrassed enough already in front of the handsome stranger. He was apt to think her a deranged oaf. "I happened to fall into the street in front of your house." That wasn't exactly a lie. She did fall into the street that ran in front of Montague House.

A shudder rippled through her petite sister. "Pray, Thompson, run and fetch the surgeon." Turning to Georgiana, she added, "Do you think you've broken something?"

"It's probably just a bruise. You must own, I am possessed of strong bones. None of my falls have ever resulted in a broken bone."

The countess's gaze moved to the handsome man, her brows hiked in query.

"Allow me to introduce myself, my lady. I am Lord Churston. I was at hand when your sister's unfortunate accident occurred."

"He carried me. It's a pity I'm not as light as you." Lucy was the only Beresford female not considered a beauty, partially because of her excessive slenderness.

"You were feather light, Miss Beresford," he said gallantly.

"How do you know my name?"

"Your footman addressed you, but I had already deduced your name when I learned your sister was the new Lady Montague. Everyone knows Monty wed one of the lovely Beresfords."

Georgiana felt her cheeks turn scarlet.

"My sister really is quite lovely," Lucy said, "when she's not covered in mud."

His gaze swept over Georgiana. "I know." Lord Churston then faced Georgiana. "May I call on you tomorrow to see how you're feeling?"

Her heartbeat accelerated. It was impossible to stifle the smile his request had produced. She would have the opportunity to see him again—when she could endeavor to make a better impression upon the Paragon. "That's very kind, my lord. I shall be delighted to receive you."

He bowed. "I hope you will give me a positive report then."

As he strode from the chamber, she called out, "Thank you so much for . . . for everything today."

He turned back and flashed her a disarming smile. "It was my pleasure."

Once he had descended the stairs, Lucy said, "What an extraordinarily handsome fellow! I dare say it would be worth an injury to fall into his arms. You must tell me everything, but let's first get you into clean clothes."

Lucy rang for Peg and instructed her to bring Georgiana fresh clothing, and Thompson returned with a message that the surgeon should be in attendance within the hour.

They closed the drawing room doors, and, with help, Georgiana stood and disrobed. She, Lucy, and Peg all looked at her swollen thigh.

"Yer gonna be black and blue tomorrow," Peg said.

Lucy nodded. "At least there's no bone sticking out. Does it hurt to put weight on that leg?"

"Actually, it does."

"We'll have the footman carry you up to your bedchamber in a sedan chair. After we see the surgeon." Lucy withdrew a handkerchief from her pocket and blew her dainty nose.

Georgiana was relieved she wouldn't be finding herself hoisted into more men's arms. Though being carried by Lord Churston had been rather pleasant. If only she'd not looked like a drowned beggar woman.

"What else hurts?" Lucy asked.

"I'm sore everywhere. I tried to brace my fall with my hands, and my wrists are sore. See, even though I was wearing gloves, they're red and sting-y."

Lucy frowned at them.

Once Georgiana was cleaned up, Lucy sat, blew her nose once more, and asked, "Pray, tell me, how did you end up lying in the muddy street?"

Georgiana sighed. "I confess, I was on my way to see Harriett—"

"Alone?"

"It's only a two-minute walk—surrounded by masses of people. I was perfectly safe."

Lucy glared. "So you say, but I see otherwise."

"I have to tell you I saw the most extraordinary sight. That's what made me fall in the street."

"What?"

"I'm certain I saw Mrs. Powell."

"Who the devil is Mrs. Powell?"

"Oh, I forgot. You don't know her. Remember when I was fourteen and recovering from lung fever, our parents sent me to that school in Devon, thinking the warming climate there would help me recover more quickly?"

"Yes."

"Well, a Mrs. Powell, who was married to a clergyman, came twice a week to instruct us on the pianoforte."

"So what's so extraordinary about seeing her in London?"

"Mrs. Powell is dead. I went to her funeral."

CHAPTER TWO

C HARLES, VISCOUNT CHURSTON, was thankful today's skies were clear. He did not wish to call on Miss Beresford sporting soaked clothing and wet hair. He was also thankful the clouds had burst the previous day prior to that lady's outing. Had it not been for the wet pavement, he would never have had the opportunity to come to her rescue after the unfortunate fall— though he did most sincerely hope the beauty had not been seriously injured.

Through his looking glass, he was able to observe Thorne's skillful tying of his freshly starched, snowy white cravat. "The gray coat today, Thorne."

His valet's brows rose. His valet knew him too well. Charles never wore the gray to his typical gentlemanly pursuits like sparring at Jackson's studio, or wagering on the cock fights, or attending the racing meetings. The gray was reserved for more fashionable events. Like visiting the lovely Miss Beresford.

The door to his bedchamber burst open, and the Honorable Freddie Fortescue came strolling into the bedchamber as if he were master here. In actuality, he spent almost as much time at his best friend's house as its master did. Like the master, Freddie never had to be announced. His welcome was always assured.

"Good day to you," Charles said, standing as his man assisted him into the gray coat.

Freddie squinted at his friend. "Bit fancy for going to Tatt's, ain't you?"

"We're not going to Tattersall's."

"We ain't? Then where in the devil are we going?"

"We're going to Montague House to pay a call on the most beautiful creature in the three kingdoms."

"I know Monty's got a pack of sisters but don't remember any of them being noted for their beauty."

"It's not his sister. It's his new wife's sister."

"A Beresford?"

"Indeed. You remember James Beresford from Eton?"

His face puzzled, Freddie said, "What's he got to do with us going to Montague House?"

"Can you not recall when we were lads and some of our family members came to observe our cricket match?"

"Indeed, I do. Me grandfather, the Earl of Morely, came to watch, though I was woefully disappointing."

"You were not disappointing," Charles said. "You performed your tasks admirably."

"My limited tasks. Hadn't thought about James Beresford in a long while. Why doesn't he come to London anymore?"

"I believe I heard he fancies agriculture. Spends all his time improving his estates."

Freddy's face screwed up in thought. "Does he not own something like a fourth of England?"

"Something like that. Anyway, can you not recall that his sister came to Eton that day? I learned later her name was Georgiana. She was without question the prettiest girl I'd ever seen."

Freddie's lips pursed. "Don't recall. I was oblivious to petticoats in those days."

"I wasn't aware that petticoats were in my line at that time, but I was much taken with her beauty and have never forgotten her. Perceive, if you will, my delight when I saw her walking along the pavement at Piccadilly yesterday."

He paused as he pictured her. Though her figure of average proportions was perfection, it was her flawless face that commanded attention. Large eyes in a muted blue-green softened her incomparable features, and when she smiled, stunning white teeth took backstage to the dimples which indented the sweep of her fair cheeks. To be favored by one of her room-brightening smiles was better than a win at Faro.

"I was honored to be able to come to her assistance when she tumbled on the slick pavement."

The shocked look Freddie directed at him made Charles wonder if a giant insect had landed upon his head. His friend's mouth gaped open. His eyes widened. "Do not tell me you picked her up and carried her along the street!"

"How did you know?" Charles asked.

"I read it in this morning's *Gazette*. It's a most shocking account."

"Nothing whatsoever was shocking about it. Leave it to the *Gazette* to make something sinister out of a gentlemanly action. Why do you even subscribe to that piece of rubbish?"

"It's far more interesting than Parliamentary accounts or manifests of ships. There's lots of useful information there."

"Give me one example."

"I certainly will. That buxom little opera dancer with the black hair is no longer under the protection of Lord March. Been thinking I might fancy her now that Mrs. Baddeley's lost her front tooth. Can't abide a woman with gap in the front."

"You're very shallow."

"You wouldn't think your Miss Beresford so bloody beautiful if she lost her front tooth!"

"I'm sure she'd still be beautiful. Now, go fetch your copy of today's *Gazette*. I must see what those scandalmongers are saying about the unblemished Miss Beresford."

During the fifteen minutes it took his friend to get the newspaper—which Charles hated to dignify by calling it a newspaper—Charles paced the floor of his library, seething with anger. He gave much thought to filing a lawsuit against the *Gazette*. Anything to preserve the lady's good name. But the more he considered that prospect, the more he realized such an action would cast the innocent victim into notoriety, and he would never do anything to hurt her or to expose her to potential censure.

When Freddie returned, Charles snatched the paper and raced to the window where the light was best for reading.

Shocking Display of Affection on London's Busiest Street in Daylight

Who was the tall man who took such liberties with Miss Georgiana Beresford, cousin to the Earl of Devere and sister-in-law of the Earl of Montague, yesterday?

In front of innumerable onlookers, the tall gentleman lifted that unmarried young woman into his arms, whereupon the maiden threw her arms around the man's neck in a most amorous fashion.

The happy gentleman proceeded to stroll along Piccadilly Street, a smile on his face. One wonders what perceived delights awaited the man once he had the scandalous Miss Beresford behind closed doors.

Nausea expanded and rose into his chest as he read the disgusting lies and innuendo about yesterday's well-intended act. He prayed the poor lady's family did not subscribe to that outrageous *Gazette*. He threw it into the fire and began to storm from the chamber.

"I don't believe I want to go to the lady's house with you," Freddie said.

"You're coming." Freddy, the dear fellow that he was, had always been a most obliging friend.

"Why must I?"

"Because there's respectability in numbers."

"Oh," Charles's simple-minded friend said.

➤➤➤❰❰❰

"I'M GRATEFUL YOU didn't break anything," her sister said to Georgiana.

"I'm grateful the surgeon said I'd be walking normally in a week." She eyed Lucy through the looking glass above her dressing table. "I'm actually better today—after lying in my bed for fourteen straight hours."

"I don't know why you had to get up and don clothing. You're certainly not going anywhere."

"I have a perfectly good reason for getting dressed in my new green frock."

"And that would be . . . ?"

"Lord Churston said he would call on me today. I must look my best."

Lucy directed an amused look at her. "I declare, I do believe you fancy the gentleman! I was beginning to think you were going to follow in our cousin Lady Sophia's footsteps and spurn seven-and-forty suitors before finding your perfect mate. How many offers of marriage did you reject last Season?"

Georgiana glared. "Only five—and you must own, none of them would be considered a matrimonial prize."

Lucy put hands to hips and glared back. "Lord Renshaw's a marquess and is owner of the finest house in all of Northumberland."

"And I never had to spurn him. I merely put as much distance between us as possible so it wouldn't come to that. But were he a duke, I wouldn't have had him. Lord Renshaw's enthusiasm for angling resulted in the fellow always smelling of fish. I couldn't tolerate the stench."

"I can see why you'd not wish to kiss such a man."

"I could kiss Lord Churston."

"I asked Monty about him last night, and he he said Lord Churston was a fine fellow."

"There you have it! He must be a fine fellow if my brother-in-law deems it so, though I could have told you that. He's unquestionably the most gallant man I've ever had the pleasure of meeting."

Peg put pearl clips in Georgiana's hair to complete her toilette, and it was none too soon for the footman tapped on the door and announced a Lord Churston and Honorable Mr. Fortescue requested to see Miss Beresford.

"Show them to the drawing room," Lucy instructed, "then bring the sedan chair to carry my sister to that chamber."

The two gentlemen stood when the ladies entered the drawing room. A pair of footmen bearing the sedan chair helped Georgiana to the sofa near the hearth. As hostess, Lucy remained standing and greeted the gentlemen.

Both men looked to be of the same age—which Georgiana would put in the late twenties—and both dressed well. Lord Churston stood several inches taller than the man accompanying him. While others might find the other man to be handsome, no man could compare to Lord Churston in Georgiana's eyes.

An indefinable quality about him elevated him over all other men of her acquaintance, especially the men who had previously been her suitors. He was not handsome in the classic sense, though his body could not have been improved upon. The man's raw masculinity was tempered by a tenderness absent in most other men. The effect he had upon her was as unexpected as it was undeniable. She had heard of love at first sight but had never thought to experience it.

Until now.

The viscount came to Lucy, lowered head into a bow, and mock kissed her hand. "Thank you, Lady Montague, for allowing us into your house. May I present my friend, the Honorable Frederick Fortescue?"

She dipped a curtsey as the second man brushed his lips above her outstretched hand.

Then Lord Churston faced Georgiana. "I've come to learn of

the report you received from the surgeon." His gaze whisked over her left leg. "I'm happy to see he did not have to set any bones."

"And I'm happy to report I'm much improved already today. No broken bones, just bruising." She relayed the good news from the surgeon as Lucy came to sit on the opposite end of the sofa from her.

"Pray, gentlemen," Lucy said, "select a chair and be seated."

There was an awkward silence for a moment before Georgiana said, "I take it Mr. Fortescue is your friend?"

"Indeed," Lord Churston said. "We've been friends since Eton."

"Did you two know my brother?" she asked, eyeing his lordship's friend.

"James?" Mr. Fortescue looked to his friend.

"James Beresford from Eton."

"Oh, yes. Fine fellow. Don't see him in London anymore."

"He actually came down for my recent wedding to Lord Montague," Lucy said.

"I recall reading something about Lord Montague and a Miss Beresford saving the life of the Duke of Wellington. That was you?" Mr. Fortescue asked Lucy.

"Indeed it was."

Mr. Fortescue continued addressing Lucy. "The Beresfords have certainly become an adventurous bunch."

"Those days are over. All my cousins are now happily wed, and I am, too."

"Well, there's your sister here. Plenty of trouble for her to get into. Just read the *Gazette*." As soon as Mr. Fortescue spoke, it was obvious he'd said something he was not supposed to mention.

Georgiana's gaze flicked to his friend.

Anger surged into Lord Churston's face as he glared at his friend.

"What is your friend referring to, my lord?" Georgiana asked.

Lord Churston drew a deep breath. "One should never believe what one reads in the *Gazette*."

"Monty refuses to read it," Lucy said.

Georgiana stared at Lord Churston. How could such a kindly man be so quickly transformed by anger?

A commotion came from downstairs, followed by feet pounding up the stairs. Georgiana turned to the room's doorway, and her cousin Devere stood there, every bit as angry looking as Lord Churston. In his hand, he held a newspaper. "What the devil is the meaning of this?" His eyes locked with Georgiana's.

"Is that the *Gazette*?" she asked.

He angrily strode to her and threw it on her lap.

The two gentlemen callers rose and issued a terse greeting to her angry cousin, who was the head of the Beresford family.

On the top left side of today's front page, she read the article about the "Shocking Display of Affection." And indeed she was shocked.

Lord Churston addressed Devere. "It's lies. Your cousin fell and was injured. I am the man who carried her here. She did not put her arms around me. She didn't even know me."

"Yet now she's ruined, and I don't know how we can ever restore her good name," Devere said.

"I do." Lord Churston's anger vanished, and he offered Georgiana a soft smile. "The injured lady was merely being carried by her future husband."

CHAPTER THREE

E VER SINCE CHARLES had seen that wicked article in the *Gazette*, he had been trying to come up with some manner of redeeming the lady's reputation. The idea of marrying her just popped into his head, and he'd blurted it out without giving it any thought.

It was not like Charles to act impulsively. He was the kind of fellow who gave considerable care to the selection of a new coat. Yet, here he was offering for a woman who hadn't spoken more than a dozen words to him.

Marriage was a monumental decision. Marriage was for a lifetime. He'd given no more thought to the selection of his life's partner than the average man did to his choice of Madeira over brandy.

In spite of the spontaneity of his declaration, he had no regrets. He could not say the prospect of marrying the beautiful Miss Beresford was in any way unsatisfactory. Quite the opposite. She was the most appealing woman he'd ever encountered.

There was nothing objectionable about her. Being a member of the illustrious Beresford family only enhanced her desirability. His mother, who put great stock in aristocratic bloodlines, would be delighted.

But his declaration did expose him to ridicule—and potential humiliation. What if Miss Beresford laughed at him? What if she publicly rejected him? Freddie launched into a coughing fit. Devere stared at him. Lady Montague stared at him. And Miss Beresford stared at him as if he were an escapee from Bedlam. He could not have felt more vulnerable were he standing there naked.

"You're the man who carried Georgiana?" Devere asked.

"Yes."

"I didn't know you were courting my cousin."

"He's not," Georgiana Beresford said.

Charles's gut plunged. *She's going to refuse my offer.* He fully expected her to break into convulsive laughter. If he were going to be rejected, he'd rather it not occur among these onlookers. He cleared his throat. "I beg a private moment with Miss Beresford."

Her sister got up. She, Devere, and Freddie all left the chamber.

Which left Charles standing there facing Miss Beresford. He spoke first. "Forgive me for putting you in such an awkward situation."

"It's I who should be asking your forgiveness. It was incredibly kind of you to sacrifice yourself to save my honor."

"But it's my regrettable act which has potentially tarnished your good name."

"I'm sorry you regret the act."

He moved to the sofa and sat beside her. "I assure you I have no regrets. I'd do it all over again."

"It was very kind of you. Still, you don't have to be forced into marriage. I have confidence Devere can think of a way for the newspaper to expunge that wicked article."

"No one was forcing me. I offered of my own free will." Charles shrugged. "My mother's been pestering me to marry and secure the succession. I'm the only son. And . . ." He lifted her hand and pressed it within his. "It would not be a sacrifice to be married to you."

To say any more would be like cutting open his chest and

offering his heart. He needed to preserve his pride at least a little.

Being this near to her affected him palpably. Peering into her flawless face only reinforced his opinion of her simple beauty. Yesterday he'd thought her eyes blue. Today they were the pale green of a daffodil's leaf, her skin as white and smooth of an unfurling lily, her scent that of a spring bouquet. In that instant he knew he could happily spend the rest of his life with this woman.

It was a revelation which he could not give voice to. Besides opening him up to potential humiliation, admitting to his weakness for her could emasculate him. It was better that she did not know the powerful hold she had over him.

Her silence made him nervous. "I would not wish to force you into . . . an alliance that would be distasteful to you," he said. "It's your decision to make, and I shall not be offended if you decide against my offer." For some unfathomable reason, he continued grasping her hand.

She squeezed it. "It's not distasteful to me."

Did that mean she accepted his offer? His heart began to soar. He waited a moment to see if she would clarify. Or retract her statement. Then, when she said nothing more, he continued. "Will you allow me to announce the betrothal to your family members?"

She nodded shyly, her smile accentuating her delightful dimples.

In his happiness, he was powerless not to lower his head and settle his lips tenderly upon hers. How he wanted to deepen the kiss, but the girl needed time to become accustomed to him. And his kisses. And so much more.

They needed time to get used to the idea of marrying.

He cupped her face. "I'll return tonight—after you've hopefully gotten used to this unexpected proposal, and we'll discuss our future."

She favored him with a smile as he got up and fetched the others. Once they had returned to the chamber, he said, "Miss Beresford has made me the happiest man in the kingdom by consenting to become my bride."

IT WAS SHE who was the happiest person in the kingdom. She had come to London in the hopes of meeting the man of her dreams, and she'd found him after falling onto the muddied cobbles of Piccadilly. She was beginning to believe that tumble was the luckiest thing that had ever happened to her. From the moment she clapped eyes on Lord Charles Churston—she'd looked him up in *Debrett's* last night—she'd come to believe in love at first sight.

More good fortune had smiled upon her in the form of that ridiculous article in this morning's *Gazette*. Would her dear Lord Churston ever have offered for her if that wildly embellished account had not appeared in the paper?

The smile never left her face when his lordship announced their betrothal. Lucy, too, had smiled when she gazed at her sister and winked.

"I know I'm titular head of the family," Devere said, but I think James needs to deal with the marriage settlements and such for his own sisters."

"Indeed he does," Lucy said. "I shall summon him to London myself and dispatch the letter today. He needs to be here."

Devere turned to the two other men, "Gentlemen, shall we repair to Brook's? I, for one, wish to toast this alliance between our families, Churston."

As soon as the gentlemen left, Lucy came to sit beside her. "Are you certain this is what you want? You don't have to marry the man because of what was written in the *Gazette*, you know."

"I have no doubts that Lord Churston is my fate. From the moment I met him, I knew he was The One. I'm aware he only offered for me out of gallantry, but I mean to do everything in my power to make him fall in love with me."

"I will own he is very gallant. I expect the man's already fallen in love with you."

"Men aren't like us. Their racing meetings, and Parliament, and shooting—all those manly pursuits take precedence in their minds over falling in love." Georgiana sighed. "Can you give me some tips on how to make the man fall in love with me? You've certainly captivated Lord Montague."

A dreamy look came over Lucy's face. "I don't think I did anything in particular to gain Monty's love. And it was nothing like love at first sight, I assure you. It was just being together and sharing the same goals that bonded us. That will happen for you and Lord Churston, too."

Georgiana had feared Lucy would never marry because she was not considered a beauty, but Lord Montague—even if he hadn't loved Lucy at first sight—had fallen deeply in love with his delicate wife and never tired of being her protector.

Is that how Georgiana had triumphed with Lord Churston? Her injury and helplessness yesterday must have brought out a protective impulse in him.

Lucy patted her arm and stood. "I'm going to dash off a letter to that brother of ours."

ONCE THEY'D TOASTED the upcoming nuptials at the gentleman's club that was the Whigs' bastion, Devere left them. As was his custom, Freddie helped himself to more brandy, but Charles declined. He'd never been fond of drinking in the daytime.

Freddie gave his friend a quizzing look. "Why didn't you tell me you were going to offer for the girl?"

"I didn't know it myself."

"It's not too late to cry off. James Beresford hasn't drawn up the contracts."

Charles eyed his friend. "Strangely, I don't want to."

"I'm still in shock. I'm going to lose my best friend."

"No, you're not," Charles said with an affirmative shake of his head. "Nothing will change between us when I marry."

"She'll replace me. That girl's bewitched you."

"You may be right, but I won't allow the lady to know just how truly I care for her."

"Why? Said yourself you're in love with her. I dare say you've worshipped her since that day at Eton."

"I dare say you're right."

"You should tell her," Freddie said. "Can't start marriage with a lie."

"I don't plan to lie. I just won't let her know the depths of my feelings."

Freddie cleared his throat. "You are going to . . . you know?"

Charles's brows lowered. "No, I don't."

"Well, you know—*tup*."

The very idea of making love to Georgiana stirred him. "That is what a man does with his wife, is it not?" He might be speaking with authority, but in reality, Charles would not rush anything with the delicate Georgiana. Especially with her injury. As much as he longed to lie with her, he must be patient and wait for her to initiate any lovemaking.

The more he thought about it, the harder he grew.

Freddie directed another quizzing look at Charles. "What the devil was Devere talking about when he said he was the tit of the family? I thought he was a happily married man."

Sometimes it was difficult to follow Freddie's line of inquiry. Was he insinuating that Devere, a most masculine man, was a backgammoner? Then he recalled Devere's mention that he was titular head of the family. "He's the *titular* head of the family, meaning he's the title bearer, but he is not guardian to his cousins. Their brother is more than capable of acting on behalf of his sisters."

"I'll say. He's one of the wealthiest men in the kingdom, as is Devere. You've done well for yourself. I'd wager Miss Beresford has a hefty dowry."

"I would have offered for her were she a penniless orphan."

"It can't hurt that she's also a beauty. I'll give you that, old fellow."

His impending possession of the most perfect creature could not come too soon. This woman was becoming his torment. A blessed torment.

KNOWING THAT LORD Churston was going to call on her that night, Georgiana—with Peg's help—dressed in her loveliest gown of soft sky-blue muslin. Its bodice dipped low enough to leave no doubt of her gender. Once her hair had been swept back to perfection, a pair of sturdy footmen carried her to the drawing room. She came early because she was embarrassed for his lordship to see her being carried in a sedan chair like an elderly invalid.

Lucy had assured her the two would be permitted to be alone. Georgiana stretched out her sore leg on the sofa and attempted to read by the light of an oil lamp. Everyone was talking about how interesting the volume of *Lord Chesterfield's Letters to His Son* was. Until now, she had found the letters most amusing, as well. Tonight, though, she could not recall a single word she'd read. Her jumbled thoughts centered on one well-muscled, long-legged viscount.

When Lord Churston was announced, her heartbeat began to drum. Whatever would she find to say? They knew nothing about each other, yet here they were agreeing to spend the rest of their lives together. He'd said they would discuss their future. Everything had occurred so fast, she felt as if all of this was happening to someone else, almost as if a stranger had taken over her body.

He came strolling into the chamber dressed in all-black evening finery and bearing a nosegay of delicate flowers of yellow and white. "Good evening to you, Miss Beresford."

She took the flowers and sniffed at the sweet fragrance. "Thank you, but I suppose you can call me by my Christian name. Georgiana."

"And my name is Charles."

She wouldn't admit she'd already looked him up in *Debrett's*.

She scooted over to make room for him. Today's kiss had been her first. While it had caught her off guard and left her shaken, she thought she would like to repeat it. Throughout the afternoon, her insides fluttered at the memory of its magical effect upon her. She patted the cushion, and he took the seat beside her.

"Has your sister dispatched the letter to your brother?" he asked.

"Yes. We hope he'll be here by week's end. It will likely be a mixed blessing for him. He'll have married off two of his three sisters. Now we females can relieve him of the task of marrying off our youngest sister."

"Tomorrow I'll initiate steps to get a special license."

She drew in a deep breath. "You mustn't feel obliged to offer for me because of that horrid piece in the *Gazette*. Are you certain you want to go through with this marriage?"

"Yes, I'm sure. Are you?"

Her breath caught when she peered into his amber eyes. "I was hoping to find a husband this season, and I'm fortunate to have received an offer from an exceedingly honorable man."

"I realize we're strangers. It was similar with my parents. Theirs was an arranged marriage, but their parents did very well in matching them. They grew to love each other deeply."

Her chest fluttered, expanded, and soared. To love deeply was exactly what she wanted in this life. "Lord Montague says you're a fine fellow, and I have great respect for my sister's husband's opinion. I don't feel as if I'll be marrying a wife-beater."

He chuckled in a deep, masculine manner. Everything about him oozed with masculinity. "I give you my word you will be treated with the utmost respect."

"I know."

"There's another matter we need to discuss."

Her brows rose.

"About the bedchamber arrangements."

Color climbed into her cheeks. Her pulse accelerated.

He enclosed her hand in his and spoke softly. "I do want you to become my wife in every way, and it's my hope that we will have children. But I don't want to . . . to rush into intimacy you're not comfortable with. We'll wait until you come to my bed-chamber of your own will. How old are you?"

"Twenty."

"You're still very young."

She smiled. "You're just four years older than me."

"How did you know that?"

She'd have to confess now. "I looked you up in *Debrett's*."

He squeezed her hand "I'm cognizant of your innocence."

He meant her lack of lovemaking experience. Had he been disappointed in her kissing ability? Could his lack of interest in bedding her be because he already had a ladybird seeing to his manly appetites? The very notion of him making love to another woman made her feel strangely bereft.

It was difficult to read his meaning. Was he wanting to marry her merely because she was a member of the highly respected Beresford family? Could he need the generous dowry she would bring to marriage? Or did he merely wish to possess a beautiful wife—for she knew she was considered a beauty. Was she to be nothing more than an ornament to him? Did she not appeal to him? "I suppose we can let nature take its course," she managed in a feeble voice.

He nodded. "I wrote to my mother about our marriage. Actually, it was to both of my parents, but my father is not always cognizant of things. He's quite a bit older than my mother and not in good health. She never leaves his side, so she won't be able to make the journey for the wedding."

"She must be a devoted wife."

"She is."

"I look forward to meeting your mother."

His gaze sifted to her leg. "How's the injury?"

"I had trouble sleeping last night because I couldn't get comfortable, but it's been better today. If Lucy weren't being such a hovering mother hen, I'd try to walk on it. She insists I rest it at least one more day."

"Your sister's a wise woman."

"She is rather clever."

"I'm sure all the Beresfords are. As I recall, James was a dedicated learner."

She laughed. "My brother is possessed of an obsessive personality. Whatever his newest interest is, he takes excessively seriously. And he does do everything well. Except gamble. Though his losses there were not for lack of trying all his theories on probability. Poor dear. The perfectionist in him was sadly disappointed to encounter something that was out of his control. Speaking of which, do you enjoy gambling?" Though she'd doubted they would have anything to discuss, she was pleased they were taking this time to get to know each other better.

"I don't enjoy losing. Therefore, I enjoy play but only for modest stakes."

"I think that's admirable." But might it mean he couldn't afford high-stakes play? Was that why he was anxious to marry her? To get her fat dowry?

"Lord Montague tells me you're a temperate man."

"Like your brother, I like to be in control." He paused and then added, "Though I shan't try to control my wife."

My wife. How she adored the sound of it! She mustn't act too clingy, though. He needn't know how thoroughly she worshipped him. "And I shan't try to control you, my lord."

He lifted her chin. "Charles."

"Yes, Charles," she whispered.

He hauled her against him and claimed her mouth. This kiss

compared to the last like fire to ice. She found herself wrapping her arms around him and not daring to break away from anything that gave her such intense pleasure. This connection might have begun with their lips but seared through her to settle low in the torso. She dreamily clung to him, oddly feeling as if she'd infused herself with an entire bottle of champagne.

In the midst of this intoxicating experience, one coherent thought rang through her lust-fogged mind. One did not kiss with such passion if one did not enjoy it. That must mean he found her kisses satisfactory!

She certainly found his to be far more than satisfactory.

He finally pulled away and cradled her face. "Forgive me for my . . . exuberance. I must commend whoever taught my future wife how to kiss."

"That would be you," she said softly.

He groaned but said nothing. She could not understand what she could have done to provoke a groan.

"I said we'd discuss our future tonight. I would like to have been able to take our wedding trip to Stamford Hall, but my parliamentary duties will have to take priority. Do you mind starting our marriage in London?"

"Of course not. I was anxious to come to London. I adore London. Will you permit me to tour your house before we are wed?"

"*Our* house. I would take you there tomorrow if it weren't for your injury."

"It wouldn't require very much walking. Could you call? If I'm improved, I should love to go see it."

"Of course." He stood. "Then I bid you good night. Expect me at one tomorrow."

The night was so early. She wondered where he was going next. Would he be flying to the arms of his ladybird?

CHAPTER FOUR

A S HE DROVE his phaeton the short distance to Montague House the next day, Charles vowed not to kiss his fiancée today. Her kisses had far too provocative an effect upon him. When he'd left her last night, only a swim in the frigid Thames could have cooled his raging desire.

Their marriage could occur none too soon for him. How long would it take before he could lie with the intoxicating woman who'd claimed the heart he hadn't known he possessed? His breath quickened at the thought of her: soon to be his Georgiana. His love.

When he arrived at Montague House, Georgiana was seated at a chair in the entry corridor, fully dressed with woolen pelisse in royal blue and a bonnet with a matching blue sash tied around her pretty head. She leapt up and bestowed a smile on him.

"You can put weight on your leg?"

"Somewhat. Of course, you're going to carry me to and from your conveyance."

His brows lowered, and he was about to protest because of how it might look after that dreadful article in the *Gazette*, but before he could speak, she started giggling.

At the sight of her dimples and chalk-white teeth, he, too, began to laugh. "You minx!"

"You've found me out. I do hope you weren't expecting a

demure and weak wife, for I assure you, you will be sorely disappointed in me."

He came to sling his arm around her. "Never."

When they reached his phaeton, he did hoist her up, but only to her seat in the phaeton, and then he took his own seat next to her. "I wish I could have offered you sunshine." Instead it was a cold and dreary day—just what one would expect in February. His home on Berkeley Square wasn't far.

"The other day when you fell, I saw no one I know," he said. "I've been wracking my mind to think who could have been so malicious toward you. Did you see anyone you knew? I'd like to learn the identity of the evil person who set out to destroy my future wife with that piece in the *Gazette*."

"No, I didn't see anyone I know." She paused a moment. "Except for a ghost."

His hands holding the ribbons stilled as he slid a glance at her. "A ghost?"

"Yes. Sort of. That's why I fell. I was so shocked. I tried to run after her."

"After the ghost? A female ghost?" His eyes narrowed.

"Allow me to explain. Do you recall seeing a stunning beauty dressed in purple? Or actually lavender, but I know men aren't good with colors."

He shook his head. "The only beauty I saw was you."

"That's very kind of you. Did you perchance notice a carriage of the nobility waiting outside the glovemaker's?"

"No. As I said, I only had eyes for Georgiana Beresford."

"I do believe I'm going to enjoy being married to you even if you are an excessive flatterer."

"Tell me about your ghost."

"During the year I went to school in Devon—for my health after surviving lung fever—I had an exceedingly beautiful pianoforte instructor named Mrs. Powell. She was newly married to a clergyman." Georgina's face screwed up with concern. "She and her husband died when their house burned. I attended their funeral."

"I think I see where you're going with this. The beautiful woman in lavender—and I do know what lavender is—looked exactly like your Mrs. Powell."

Georgiana's eyes shimmered. "You, sir, must be terribly clever."

"I don't think she was a ghost."

"I think you're right. I never have believed in them."

"How long ago did your Mrs. Powell die?"

She shrugged. "Five or six years ago."

"The woman in lavender likely bears a strong resemblance to your Mrs. Powell, who you haven't seen in several years."

"The resemblance was so similar. I particularly wished to see the color of her eyes because Mrs. Powell's were so unusual, and this woman's eye color was the very same. An unusually pale shade of blue, similar to my sister Lucy's, and you must own, Lucy's eyes are extraordinary."

"Lucy, I take it, is Lady Montague?" He had noticed her sister's lovely eyes.

"Yes. And Mrs. Powell's were very much like Lucy's—but even more striking." She shook her head. "Our eyes met, and I truly believed the woman in lavender recognized me. I know that sounds ridiculous."

"So that's why you fell onto the street? You were charging to her coach?"

"Yes. I do wish I'd paid more attention to the coach. Are you sure you didn't see it?"

"Sorry."

"I can't be sorry, not when you said you only had eyes for me. How flattering that even in the presence of the stunning Mrs. Powell double, you only looked at me. Pray, don't think me egotistical, but I'm fully aware others find me attractive in a wholesome way. But nothing about me could come close to the sensuality of the exotically beautiful Mrs. Powell. I'm still stunned you didn't notice her—or are you merely saying that to make me feel good?"

"I didn't notice anyone on that pavement except you." He turned onto Berkeley Square. "Can you guess which of these houses is to be your future home?"

She pointed to the largest house on the square. "It can't be that one for I know it belongs to Lord and Lady Jersey. All the houses are very nice. I am incapable of trying to pick yours out because, quite honestly, I know so little of you or your family. Are you well off or not?"

"Not. My father's still alive. I will receive control of the property upon his death, which I hope does not occur until I'm a very old man."

"Which, unfortunately, is not likely, as you mentioned he is unwell?"

It was difficult for him to speak of. He was close to his father, who'd always been loving and generous to him. All he could do was nod as he pulled to a stop opposite the square from the Jerseys' opulent mansion.

⋙⋘

HER FUTURE HOME was neither as grand as the Jerseys' nor as slender as the most modest house on the square. In size, the red-brick mansion was average—much the same size of Lord Montague's.

He lifted her down from the box. "Lean on me and try not to put weight on your leg."

They climbed two steps to the front door. It was in need of a fresh coat of paint. It made perfect sense that a bachelor not too far removed from his days at Oxford would have no interest in the maintenance of his house, and she understood his parents were in no position to do so while the father was probably dying far away from London.

But the negligence could indicate that money was tight, that he might have a grave need to marry a well-fixed woman like her who would bring a sizable dowry to the marriage.

Still, he had won her over—though she needed no winning over—when he'd ignored the woman who looked like the fabulously beautiful Mrs. Powell because he was taken with Georgiana's beauty.

"I keep but a skeleton staff here, as the heart of our servant staff followed my parents to Stamford. I don't have visitors, nor do I host dinners." To her surprise, he withdrew a key and opened his front door. "I also don't have a footman. The poor fellow would have no duties to perform."

They came into the entry corridor that featured the staircase with its shiny brass handrail. At night it would be lighted from a large, brass chandelier that was suspended just above the ground floor. Her gaze went to the old family portraits that staggered along the walls of the staircase. "One day I'll know the subject of each of those portraits."

She felt as if she were on the precipice of her adult life, a life where every milestone would be shared with the man who now stood beside her. She was powerless to suppress a smile.

"Then my mother will have to enlighten you, for I doubt if I know half of them."

"You sound just like James." She thought of how thoroughly she looked forward to adding to his family, to bearing his heir, but she mustn't allow him to know how eager she was to marry him. She was willing to wait until they knew each other better, to hopefully wait until he could honestly declare his affection for her. She prayed that day would come soon.

In spite of her lack of years, she knew herself, and she knew what she felt for him went far beyond physical attraction. During last year's Season—her first—she had become acquainted with at least a hundred men, but not a single one of them had appealed to her in the way Charles Churston did. Everything about him affected her profoundly. No other man would ever supplant him in her affections.

"My mother will have to acquaint you with all the family connections, but allow me to show you your future home. I dare say it needs a woman's care. My dear mother's been away for more than two years, and she took our capable housekeeper with her. Of course, once we're married, we'll need to fully staff this place. Should you wish to interview candidates?"

"Indeed, I would." Having a house of her own to run had always appealed to her.

Footsteps came from the basement, and a middle-aged man with thinning medium brown hair and dressed in black greeted his master. "Good day, my lord. Will you be needing anything?"

"No, my good man, but I should like to introduce you to the woman who's to be your new mistress, my future wife. My dear Miss Beresford, this is my able man-of-all-talents, Thorne."

"I look forward to seeing more of you, Mr. Thorne."

The servant bowed to her. Before he returned to the basement, he said, "Please ring, my lord, if you need me for anything."

Charles moved closer to her and proffered his arm. "Allow me to show you the library. It's my favorite chamber."

The library was located at the end of the corridor, and because it was at the back of the house, it was afforded a window which helped to brighten the dark chamber. The room's abundance of dark wood bookcases and heavy, dark furnishings was also relieved by a blazing fire in the hearth.

"At least you've got staff to see to the fires," she said. "It's been so beastly cold."

"For that, I'm thankful—for the staff and the fire, not the cold."

She stood in the doorway and surveyed the comforting chamber. The heavy draperies, like the sofa near the fire, were of asparagus green velvet, a color that was picked up again in the Turkey carpet which was predominately faded red and which covered much of the chamber's wooden floors.

Her gaze traveled to the books. While much of the library

featured an array of fine, leather-bound classics from the Greeks and Romans, at least half the shelves sagged under the weight of volumes published in the past ten to twenty years. They ranged from Byron to Wordsworth to works of history and philosophy from Gibbon and Payne. Then she remembered that, like her cousin Devere, Lord Churston was also a Whig.

"I'm guessing the newer works must have been favored by you, my—Charles." She had started to call him *my lord*.

He shrugged. "Most of them. I will add that my father and I share much the same interests."

She hoped that man who admired his father would be more likely to respect his wife. "Is your father a Whig?"

He nodded somberly. "It's a source of sadness that he's no longer able to take his seat in the House of Lords."

"As I imagine it's a source of pride for him to know you carry on his work in the House of Commons." When his father died, she knew, Charles would move to the House of Lords, but she had no desire to get too macabre. Her glance swung around the chamber one last time. "I hope to spend much time here. This chamber has great warmth, in every way."

His hand moved to her waist, and he steered her from the room and back to the front of the house to mount the stairs to the drawing room.

A servant—was it Thorne or another?—had drawn open the draperies in the generously sized drawing room. The chamber was dressed in bright lemon-yellow silks and appeared to be in good condition. Was that because it was never used?

"I took the liberty of having the parlor maid build fires here today, knowing you were coming. Normally, I just keep them in the occupied chambers."

So he had a parlor maid and his man-of-all-talents. She supposed there was a cook, also. Her eye was drawn to a Gainsborough portrait over the fireplace of a beautiful woman. The facial features of the woman in the pale blue dress looked remarkably like Charles's. She felt him watching her. "Your mother?"

"Yes."

"She's beautiful."

"She was then, and she is still, though she's much changed. Then, her powdered hair looked gray. Now, it's gray with no powder."

She smiled up at him.

"Even though we're soon to be married, I'll not permit myself to show you to your future bedchamber. I won't have it said I compromised your virtue in any way." He began to walk her back down the stairs.

Disappointment strummed through her. Not just because she had not been able to see the chambers she and her husband would occupy, but because he had no desire to be in an intimate chamber with her.

He'd already said he was not going to bed her on their wedding night.

Not being invited to see those chambers, as much as anything else, convinced her that he was bedding another woman. A woman who possibly possessed his heart but who was not worthy of his illustrious family title.

CHAPTER FIVE

"So, I'm told I'm to draw up the marriage contracts between you and a man you scarcely know."

Georgiana glared at her brother, who'd arrived late that afternoon, stunning her with his prompt arrival just days after the letter announcing her nuptials was dispatched. He had summoned her to Devere House, where he was staying. She hadn't even had the opportunity to visit with her sister, Emily, who had come with James. "Were you also told I knew the moment I saw him he was The One? But, please, don't reveal that to him when you talk to him."

"Lucy did mention something to that effect," James said. "I, of course, don't believe in love at first sight."

"Yes, I know you're terribly practical, but I do hope one day you'll know what it is to fall in love at first sight, as I have." Her voice went from argumentative to soft. "My Lord Churston is a most worthy man. You must have known him at Eton. I believe he was just behind you."

"I did, and I find nothing objectionable in him. He seems to be a fine man. Both Devere and Monty agree on that."

"Then I beg that you hurry with the settlements for I'm most anxious to marry."

His brows lowered. "Is there merit to the scandalous article in the *Gazette*? Have you been . . . compromised?"

"Certainly not! Lord Churston is an exceedingly honorable man."

"Can you explain that piece of rubbish in the *Gazette*?"

She told him everything.

"And you're certain you saw no one you know there on the pavement that day?" he asked.

"Just the ghost," she said with a nod.

"How peculiar. It does seem as if someone is bent on ruining you. I suppose I should be grateful to Lord Churston for saving your reputation. In fact, I'm taking it upon myself to have a notice of your nuptials put in all the newspapers tomorrow. That should still those wagging tongues."

"Then we can marry tomorrow?"

"Let's say the day after. It will take my solicitor a bit to finalize the legal details of your settlement. As you know, our father provided handsomely for all his daughters. Churston is a fortunate man."

Her brother was not given to speaking emotionally, but she knew he meant Charles was fortunate to win her affections—along with a hefty dowry.

"I'm the fortunate one." She stood. "I don't know why you never open up Beresford House and spend some time in London."

"Can't. Hindley's going to be demonstrating a new reaper that should revolutionize agriculture. It's exciting to be among the first to adopt these progressive farming methods."

"It would be even more exciting if you'd allow yourself to fall in love."

"There will be time for that when I'm older and desirous of starting a family, but that, I dare say, is many years away."

Eyes heavenward, she shook her head and left the chamber. She hastened to go see Emily. There was just a year between the two sisters, and in appearance, they looked almost like twins. Both were possessed of brown hair, hazel eyes, slender torsos, and remarkable dimples which never failed to solicit comments.

The younger was actually taller.

In temperament, though, the two were vastly different. Georgiana surrounded herself with friends and acquaintances and was considered outgoing. Emily, though well liked, typically preferred getting lost in the pages of a book over being in a chamber full of people.

"I cannot believe you've gone and gotten yourself betrothed!" Emily said as they hugged. "It's barely more than a week since you were with us at Tilford."

"I know it seems incomprehensible," Georgiana responded, "but you know me well enough to understand I don't easily have my head turned by a handsome man."

"I will own I was shocked. If you'd wanted to marry, you had ample opportunity last Season to have made a brilliant match. I believed you were holding out for the perfect mate, your own personal knight errant."

"And, my dear Em, that's exactly what I've found. I knew the moment I saw him. I cannot wait for you to meet him."

"I have every confidence in your decision," Emily said. "You must tell me all about your Lord Churston."

"I will. But first you're coming to stay with Lucy and me at Montague House. It's best we three sisters stay together my last few days as an unmarried woman." The very idea of being married soon, being married to her Lord Churston, filled Georgiana with joy.

LATER THAT NIGHT, Charles met with his future brother-in-law. "It's good of you to come to London," he told James Beresford after shaking his hand and taking a seat in the Devere library. It was just the two of them, face to face in armchairs at either side of the blazing fire.

"Freddie Fortescue and I were just speaking of you, Beresford. It's been quite a while since you've been in town."

"I suppose my sister's told you I stay busy looking after the family lands."

"Indeed, she has." Charles had always liked James Beresford but found him to be reserved tonight. Was he opposed to this marriage?

"The announcement of your impending marriage to Georgiana will go into all the newspapers tomorrow morning."

Relief rushed over Charles. "I'm happy it meets with your approval."

"I suppose you know my sister has ten thousand a year of her own."

Charles swallowed. He'd known the Beresford girls had fat dowries, but he'd never imagined they were *that* large. Though his ancient family was landed, even when his father departed this earth, Charles would not be that wealthy. "That's exceedingly generous."

"Our father was most indulgent—and he adored his daughters. As I hope you will. Adore Georgiana, that is. Montague has satisfied me on that score with her older sister."

"I will cherish her. I believe I may have fallen in love with her that day she came to Eton for our cricket match. Do you remember?"

"She couldn't have been more than fourteen!"

"Much too young, I know, to have designs on, but I could never forget the beauty of that wholesome face. I've carried it all these years, and when I saw her walking down Piccadilly that day, it was like being struck by lightning. Please don't tell her that, though. I shouldn't want her to think I get tossed off over juvenile girls."

James chuckled. "I do believe you'll make Georgiana a good husband." James's eyes narrowed. "You were the one who carried her that day on Piccadilly? The mystery man in the *Gazette* account?"

"I was, but your sister did nothing as improper as placing her arms around me. She didn't know me. I only helped because she was injured and unable to stand upon that leg." Charles sighed. "I'm happy to report she did not sustain any serious injuries and is able to walk without pain now."

"I keep wondering who could have known her that day, who could have set out to destroy her reputation."

"I do, too. If I ever learn, I'll be sorely tempted to meet him at dawn with pistols."

"Me, too. By the way, a portion of my sister's dowry will be set aside for your future children."

Charles's heartbeat thumped. He stood, shook James's hand, and left, his step feather light, his heart full of promise.

Two more days, and Georgiana Beresford would be his.

DURING THOSE NEXT two days, Georgiana interviewed prospective servants. She would, of course, bring Peg with her when she married, but she needed to engage a proper housekeeper, a butler, and one footman. As the wife of what she believed to be an up-and-coming member of the House of Commons, she wished to begin entertaining.

She hoped to have routs, dinners, and even salons at their home. She wanted to be a credit to her husband.

One of her first duties was to hire painters to freshen up their home's front door and trim in a glossy, fresh white.

When she had the opportunity to hire the butler and housekeeper from the late Lord Laverham's house, she took it as a sign that this marriage was being blessed. Everything was working out perfectly. The new housekeeper, one Mrs. Jones, was in her late forties and had the decades of experience to match her age. It didn't take long for Georgiana to realize Mrs. Jones was highly qualified. To make matters even more satisfactory, the woman had a pleasant countenance. The same could not be said for

Wilcox, the exceedingly formal man Georgiana engaged to be their butler, though it hadn't hurt his cause that Mrs. Jones had spoken highly of him.

Devere had told her one of his footmen had a younger brother ready to go into service, and she hired him to be their other footman. Jonathan was just seventeen but, like his brother, quite tall for his age. He was nearly as tall as Charles, and that was considerably above average.

Now that the Churstons had their staff, she hoped Charles would be satisfied with her selections.

THEY HAD CHOSEN to have a small, family wedding which took place in the drawing room at Devere House. His friend, Freddie Fortescue, stood beside Charles, and Georgiana's sister, Lucy, stood on the opposite side of the vicar. Since it was a bitterly cold February day, they stood in front of the fire. Chairs had been arranged as if in a church with a central aisle. They were occupied by Beresfords and their spouses: Lord and Lady Devere, Lord and Lady Rockingham, Lucy's husband, Lord Montague, and the youngest Beresford, Emily.

Charles turned to look when James Beresford started to escort his slightly limping sister down the makeshift aisle. His chest expanded with powerful emotions. Georgiana, his Georgiana, was more beautiful than ever. It was as if a madonna had come to earth. A simple ivory gown flowed over her smooth curves and into a demi-train. Her sable tresses were crowned with a floral wreath adorned with pearls. The perfection of her smiling face lacked only a glowing halo to confirm celestial origins.

I am the luckiest man in the kingdom.

He'd been a guest at a number of weddings but had paid little attention to the words of the ceremony. Today, every word affected him profoundly, especially *her body will become your body* and *until parted by death.* There, in the presence of the vicar, he prayed he would be granted a long life with this woman.

He had purchased a simple gold band at Rundell and Bridge for the ceremony. Later, when he saw his mother, he would exchange the band for a piece from his family's jewels. When he slipped it on her graceful finger, she smiled up at him, her cheeks dimpling. He felt as if he'd grown a foot taller.

Following the ceremony, all of them partook of a lavish wedding meal in the generously sized Devere dinner room.

CHARLES, HER HUSBAND—HOW she loved the sound of it!—passed her the stuffed quail. Their hands brushed and she looked up at him dreamily. His gaze held. Today was unquestionably the happiest day of her life.

She was disappointed they would have to stay in town for his parliamentary duties. How she would have loved to have taken a wedding trip with him. Just the two of them. They would have gotten the opportunity to get to know one another better, and she wouldn't have had to share him with anyone else. All that forced togetherness would surely have resulted in a romance, a romance she hoped would last a lifetime.

She was determined to make the best of every moment they had together.

Champagne flowed. James, who sat across from them, stood. "I offer a toast to my dear sister and her bridegroom. May their lives together be filled with every conceivable happiness."

Everyone at the table drank to them.

Devere followed. "I am pleased to welcome Lord Churston into the Beresford family. I am equally as pleased to add another Whig to our family."

They all laughed. Lord Rockingham tapped his glass to Devere's and downed his glass, as did the others.

"It's really the most amazing thing that everyone here at the table—with the exception of the Honorable Freddie Fortescue and Miss Emily Beresford—has met and married their mate during these past several months," Lady Harriett said.

"Indeed, it is," Devere said. "We Beresfords don't do anything by halves."

Lord Montague sighed. "Let us hope the Beresfords have finished with their so-called adventures."

"I will most happily drink to that," Devere said, tossing back another glass of champagne.

With all its many courses, the meal lasted throughout the afternoon. Night came early this time of year. By the time the bridal couple was ready to leave, they were obliged to ride home in the dark.

She and Charles rode in his phaeton the short distance to their new home. He pulled to a stop in front of it and turned to her. "I want to thank you for seeing to the hiring of staff. You made admirable selections."

"I was lucky." *And I was lucky to marry you.*

"Now you must redecorate whatever rooms you deem necessary. You'll probably want to start with the viscountess's chamber."

"Shall we go see it?"

CHAPTER SIX

C HARLES HAD SHREWDLY calculated when they would look at the bedchambers. By going there first, when it was too early to go to sleep, he could hopefully dispatch that task before his desire for her made him go back on his promise to wait before bedding her.

As they mounted the steps hand in hand, he cautioned himself to avoid looking at the bed. He must solicit her opinions on what needed to be done. This would take a newcomer's impartial eye.

While they were at it, she might as well offer suggestions on what to do to his father's former bedchamber, where Charles now slept. He doubted it had changed one bit in four decades.

Those closest to the gradual decay of once-lovely chambers were as unaware of the transformation as a wife failing to observe when gray replaces her husband's golden tresses, one silvery thread at a time.

"Thorne tells me his duties have been greatly reduced since your footman and butler have taken over so many of them. He's happy to return to being a valet, and truth be told, I will also. My clothing hasn't been cared for as meticulously as he used to do." He pointed to the wall sconces. "The footman has taken over the lighting of sconces and lamps, for one thing."

"He was such a dear. He told me he'd always wanted to be a

footman."

"I suppose it's better than having to work in the elements or in one of those factories with the blazing furnaces," Charles said.

"And you must own, the footmen are mostly a handsome lot."

He chuckled. "I hadn't noticed." He paused in front of a door. "This is the viscountess's chamber."

After moving into the room, he tried to look at it as one who'd never seen it before, but it was difficult. He'd always associated it with his lovely mother and, consequently, thought it a beautiful room. But now that he gave it a good critical look, he realized it had actually become shabby, though not through his mother's fault. She hadn't resided here on a daily basis in many years.

In fact, in the poignant, congratulatory letter she'd written him since he'd notified her of his nuptials, she had suggested the new viscountess redecorate the chamber. The chamber had been a pale blue, but most of its silks had faded to an indistinguishable shade of gray.

The room was even larger than his. He remembered the evenings his parents would sit on the settee before the marble fireplace, and Mama would listen to Papa rehearsing a speech he was to give in the House of Lords.

His gaze settled on the gilded escritoire with curved French legs. He could still picture his mother sitting there in some frilly feminine concoction, dashing off her abundant and never-ending correspondence.

"Oh, I must keep the escritoire!" his bride said. "It's so lovely."

He was pleased. He still refused to look at the bed.

She stood still and surveyed the chamber for a few moments before she spoke.

"Would you object if I change the colors? You must own, the draperies and bedcoverings need to be replaced. I declare, you could read a newspaper through those fragile draperies."

"I'm embarrassed. I see now that what you've noticed is true. Please have a free hand in replacing anything you wish—my mother suggested you do so."

"How kind of her. I'll have the painters back beginning tomorrow. Do you not think it best to have a completely different color than your mother had? I wouldn't want you to feel awkward." Her eyes lifted to peer at him. "Associating your wife's bed with your mother's. It must be completely different. Except I will keep the actual bed. It's lovely. Just the colors will change."

He couldn't look her in the eye. Not here. Not so close to the bed. Why had he ever told her he was willing to wait? This was his bloody wedding night! He had every right to make love to his wife! "That's a very good idea. What color do you think you'll use?"

"Pink. I've always loved pink."

He nodded his approval. "Perhaps you can do up my chambers, also. I dare say they're even more in need than this. My father was a bachelor until he married my mother at forty, and I doubt he's changed a thing there since he inherited at five-and-twenty."

They strolled from the viscountess's adjacent dressing chamber into the viscount's connecting chamber.

He could not wait for the day he could stand here with her as she disrobed. His breath caught, and he hastened to his chamber, which he'd always thought of as scarlet but which he now realized had faded into something resembling watered-down wine.

Again, he avoided looking at the bed. How he would like the next Viscount Churston to be conceived in that bed. With his wife. The notion that the beautiful Georgiana Beresford was his wife had the same effect upon him as this afternoon's champagne.

"I do believe you're right! This chamber is hideously shabby." She moved to him and spoke in a gentle voice. "Has lack of money been a problem? You must be honest with me about everything now that we're married."

"No, money's not a problem! I'm perfectly capable of paying for painters and drapers and such. I just never thought of it." He turned away from the bed and glared at her. "Disavow yourself of the notion I may have married you for your handsome dowry. I'd have married you had you been penniless." He could have thwacked himself in the head. He'd revealed far more about the depths of his feelings than he wanted to.

She cupped a warm hand against his cheek and gifted him with one of her heart-throbbing smiles. "That's the sweetest thing you could have said, my dearest."

My dearest. God help him! In addition to arousing him, she had now opened with the first gambit. Thank God!

"Well, what do you think you're going to do with this chamber?" he asked.

"The wood pieces are good. We'll just need fresh paint and new silks and velvets. Are you partial to red—though it's been centuries since this was red—or should you like to change the color?"

"I'm not married to red, *my love.* You have free rein to do whatever you want. And I can afford to pay for it." He followed her lead and referred to her as *my love*, an even stronger endearment. Things were progressing well.

Now that they'd analyzed the bedchambers, what were they to do? They'd partaken of a gargantuan meal. It was too early for sleep. He moved to the door. "Do you play chess?" he asked.

"Poorly."

He offered her a smile. "Do you fancy a game in front of the fire in the library?"

"I do. I love your library. It's so warm and comforting."

"*Our* library." He held her hand as they descended the stairs. The footman assisted him in setting up the game table in front of the fireplace. "Care for a glass of Madeira?" Charles asked.

"I shouldn't after all that champagne, but I'm foolishly weak."

He moved to the tray and removed the decanter's stopper.

"You're neither weak nor foolish."

A tap sounded on the door, and Jonathan opened it. "A Mr. Fortescue to see you, my lord."

Freddie? What the devil was he doing here? Even though the fellow knew Charles did not intend to consummate the marriage this night, he should know better than to intrude upon a man's wedding night.

Charles and Georgiana exchanged puzzled glances.

"You ought to invite him in," she said. "I dare say he wouldn't be here if it weren't important."

She obviously did not know Freddie. The man could be as dense as a rock. Charles nodded his assent.

When Freddie entered the chamber, he appeared to be hiding something behind his back. An uncharacteristic solemnity in his manner frightened Charles. This wasn't like his closest friend. "Are you all right?"

"I'm perfectly fine."

"Then?"

"You and your bride may not be so fine when you see what's been written about you in the *Gazette*. It's a demmed lie." Freddie met Georgiana's gaze. "Pardon my language, my lady."

She nodded.

Charles's stomach roiled. "Let me see it."

Georgiana had been seated at the table, but she rose and came to stand beside her husband.

Freddie unfurled the newspaper and presented it to his friend, pointing to the left-hand top of the front page. "It's on the first page again. The bloody liars." He eyed Georgiana. "Forgive my language."

"I dare say it's well warranted."

The newlyweds began to read.

It's being said the hasty marriage between a certain Lord C. and a Miss B. was orchestrated by that lady's kinsman, Lord D_v____, owing to the impending arrival of a new member to the family.

Charles's gut dropped. His hands shook with a rage he could not control. He stole a glance at his wife. Her eyes had filled with tears. He could have stood any assault on himself, but hurting Georgiana was intolerable. He wadded up the paper and thrust it back at Freddie before putting his arm around her and pulling her close. His heart bled for her.

"Why," she asked in a quivering voice, "is someone so intent on ruining me?"

Freddie puckered his lips. "You must have made a potent enemy, my lady. Who hates you so much?"

She shook her head forlornly. "I have no enemies. That I know of."

"Methinks you do," Freddie said.

Charles's hand squeezed at her waist. He wanted to haul her into his arms and embrace her, but more importantly, he needed to reassure her. "I. Will. Find. Out. Who's responsible for this! And we will demand a retraction." His words whipped out breathlessly, measured by fiery anger.

He faced her and settled hands on her shoulders. It ripped his heart to see her so distressed. "First thing in the morning, I will confront the editor of that piece of rubbish."

"If I know my brother and Devere, I expect they'll be wanting to go with you."

He nodded. "I'll go speak to them tonight." He pressed a soft kiss on her forehead, and then he and Freddie left.

CHAPTER SEVEN

G EORGIANA HAD GIVEN Peg the night off. And the next morning. She was too embarrassed to allow her maid to know about her solitary wedding night. Peg would be picturing Lord Churston removing her mistress's garments one by one on their wedding night. That same imagination would have Peg contemplating his lordship helping his wife into the day's clothing the following morning. The day *after*.

After . . . a night of lovemaking with her husband. When would that ever occur, Georgiana wondered, her spirits sinking. In so many ways Charles Churston gave every indication that he was attracted to her. Hadn't he said he'd had eyes for no one except her that day on Piccadilly? He hadn't even noticed the Incomparable doppelganger of the stunning Mrs. Powell. He seemed affectionate toward Georgiana. He'd even used endearments such as *my love* with her—turning her insides into warm butter.

But her husband's disinterest in bedding her still stung. In spite of his many kindnesses—the most significant being his generous proposal of marriage—she feared his heart already belonged to another.

Her new bedchamber was lighted by an oil lamp beside the bed as well as a blazing fire in the hearth. Somehow she managed to remove her prettiest dress without any assistance. Then, with a heavy heart, she donned the lacy white linen confection she would wear to bed.

Since it was still too early for sleep and she was too distressed for sleep anyway because of this latest attack on her character, she decided to stroll to her husband's bedchamber. He'd told her he, too, had given his man the night off, so she need not be concerned the valet would see her in her bedclothes.

When she opened the door that connected her dressing room to her husband's, her eye went straight to the bed. Would she ever lie there with him? She fleetingly thought of lying there and offering herself to him when he returned that night, but she was too timid and too ignorant of such things to make the first move. Besides, she did not want to force herself on him. She was too proud to allow him to know how foolishly attached she was to him.

Attached. What she felt for him was so much deeper than attachment. As silly as it seemed to be obsessed over someone she barely knew, she had no doubts of the depth of her love for this man who had just this very day given her his name. She allowed herself to hope that years from now, as a happy mother of Charles's children, she would look back on this peculiar wedding night with humor and a smothering dose of love.

As in her bedchamber, a lone oil lamp reposed only on one of the bedside tables, so she easily determined which side of the bed he slept on. She crossed the room and tenderly placed her hand on the pillow where his beloved head would lie. Even something that far removed from Charles had the power to accelerate her breathing.

How she missed him!

Knowing they were not going to consummate their marriage tonight, she had still expected they would spend the evening together, gawking at one another across the chess board while becoming further acquainted. Instead, because of that wretched pack of lies in the *Gazette*, she was all alone on her wedding night. Alone and miserable.

She bent over and pressed her lips to his pillow before returning to her own bedchamber. She had expected her husband would have returned by now. How long would it take for him to discuss this nasty article with her brother and cousin?

What was keeping Charles? He'd been gone for almost three hours. And Devere House was just minutes away.

Even though it wasn't to be a real wedding night, those who knew them would be expecting him to spend it with his bride. He could hardly show up at Brook's when all of London had read about their nuptials in the London newspapers.

Where was he?

Her heartbeat thudded. *He's with that other woman.* The one he's in love with.

⟫⟫⟫⟪⟪⟪

DEVERE AND JAMES were drinking port in front of the fire in Devere's library. When Charles and Freddie joined them, they looked at Charles rather as if they were viewing an apparition. Of course, no one would be expecting a bridegroom to be galivanting about London on his wedding night. Without his wife.

"My wife," Charles started, "believes you need to be apprised of this new slur against her name, though I plan to handle it tomorrow." He tossed the newspaper to James. Devere came to read over his cousin's shoulder.

"Bloody liars!" James looked disgusted.

Devere's solemn gaze met Charles's. "There's no truth in this, is there?"

"Of course not!" Charles shouted. "I've known her less than a week!"

"And I can confirm that," Freddie said, sidling up to his friend. "Can't humpity bumpity with a woman one don't know." His face collapsed when he eyed Devere and James Beresford. "Meaning no disrespect to your virtuous kinswoman."

"My sister's as innocent as a child."

"And I can also vouch for that," Charles concurred.

Devere bowed his head ruefully. "Forgive my doubting it. I know Georgiana's goodness runs deep."

"Why in the hell is some evil person bent on destroying my sister's good name?"

"I intend to discover that tomorrow," Charles said.

"How?" Devere asked.

"I'm bloody well going to march into that damned *Gazette* office and demand to know who's placing those scandalous bits of rubbish about the most perfect, wholesome, innocent woman in all of London," Charles thundered.

James and his cousin exchanged amused gazes. "I believe Lord Churston's in love with your sister, James."

James nodded. "It's a good match." James sprang to his feet. "I'm coming with you in the morning to the *Gazette* office."

Devere pursed his lips. "Someone very powerful for reasons unclear to us is determined to ruin poor Georgiana. Why?"

James shrugged. Charles shook his head woefully.

"It may be that the powerful maniac also has very deep pockets," Devere said.

"No deeper than mine, I'll vow," James said.

"Are you prepared to bribe the *Gazette*?" Devere asked.

James nodded. "I am."

Charles's lips thinned with anger. "She's my wife. I'll do the bribing."

"It's worth everything to me to see that the wretched newspaper publishes a retraction," James said.

Just picturing sweet Georgiana's fallen face when she'd read today's attack tore at Charles's heart. He'd give everything he had to force a retraction and lift away her gloom. "To me, too."

"Who's the publisher of that rubbish sheet?" Devere asked. "I hate to legitimatize it by referring to it as a newspaper."

James shook his head.

"No one respectable, that's for certain," Charles said.

"Murray will know." Devere eyed Charles. "I know it's your wedding night, old boy, but would you care to pay a visit to Murray with me tonight?"

Charles knew John Murray was one of the most respected publishers in London, though he'd never met him. "Let's go."

CHARLES'S FATHER HAD been acquainted with the elder John Murray, now deceased. He'd established the first evening newspaper in the Capital, *The Star*. John Murray II had taken his father's publishing interests a step further, launching the literary careers of some of the kingdom's most popular authors. He'd published books by Lord Byron, the lady recently revealed to be Jane Austen, and the Scottish novelist Walter Scott. His house on Albemarle Street wasn't far from Devere House.

The three visitors—for Devere had come, but Freddie had gone elsewhere—were shown to the publisher's large library while the butler fetched Mr. Murray. Charles hadn't seen so many books in one chamber since he'd been at university. The floor-to-ceiling shelves were stuffed with books, and books placed horizontally filled the gaps between the row of books and the next shelf. Every table in the lofty room held stacks of tomes, and more stacks rose from the Turkey carpet surrounding the large desk, where more books reposed.

A moment later the well-dressed publisher entered the chamber, smiling as he greeted the men and shook Devere's hand. Devere had expected an older man. This fellow was not yet forty—but far enough removed in age from Charles to have prevented their acquaintance. Devere effected the introductions between the publisher and Charles and James.

"To what do I owe the pleasure?" Murray asked, his voice that of a Scotsman.

Charles answered. "My bride is being viciously attacked in the

Gazette, and we were hoping you could tell us about its publisher."

Murray groaned. "I'm very sorry to hear this. I am afraid it's not the first time I've learned of the *Gazette's* disregard for truth." He indicated for the men to sit, then he took a seat near the fire on this blustery night. "I've never met the publisher, one Hugh Hammond. It's a bit of a mystery where he came from or how he came by the funds to launch a major newspaper."

Charles grimaced. "If one wanted to call that rubbish a newspaper."

Murray nodded. "It's often given reputable newspaper like ours a bad name."

"Do you think the newspaper might have silent partners?" Charles asked.

"I cannot verify the information, but that's what I've been told." Murray said.

"Any speculation as to who they are?" Charles asked.

Murray shook his head. "None whatsoever."

Devere eyed the publisher. "My cousin Georgiana, now Lady Churston, is a virtuous woman—still a maiden actually, as she just married today. She's being deeply vilified by the *Gazette*. Do you think we can purchase this Hammond's promise to stop printing lies about her?"

"I know the Regent has a standing payment to William Cordon to suppress any negative reports about His Royal Highness in his newspaper." Mr. Murray shrugged. "I've refused to entertain similar requests from any number of men in government."

Charles should have known such practices occurred, but to one who's inherently honest, such a revelation was disappointing. "And you have no knowledge of success in the suppression of articles in the *Gazette*?" he asked the publisher.

"I have no personal knowledge. As I said, I've never met Hammond. Knowing the Gazette's reputation, though, I'd say the likelihood of Hammond accepting bribes is very good."

"We'll meet him tomorrow," Charles said, rising, his fists

coiled with anger toward the *Gazette's* publisher.

As MUCH AS he wanted to see his bride, Charles denied himself after he dropped her brother and cousin off at Devere House. It was midnight. She would surely be asleep. At this point in their marriage, he would not feel right barging into her bedchamber while she was in bed.

There was no way he could gaze upon her reclining and not wish to take complete possession of her. He laughed bitterly to himself. He could never gaze upon her loveliness without fighting a strong desire to possess her.

But now as he drove through the dark, quiet streets of London, he could not purge from his mind the heart-wrenching vision of her when she'd read the lies in the *Gazette* earlier that evening. That perfect face, always quick to smile, had never looked more solemn. Her ever-present dimples had remained hidden, and tears had filled those remarkable eyes.

He could not bear to see the woman he loved that distraught. If only he could stay away from his house until he saw Hugh Hammond, until he'd persuaded—or paid—the vile publisher to correct the wrongs that had been directed at his beloved bride.

He wanted to be able to come to her and tell her everything had been corrected, that she would never again be harassed by the despicable press.

But not coming to her at all would not be fair. She had every right to know what had transpired tonight, even though nothing constructive had occurred. She needed to be informed of what his plans were. After all, she was at the center of everything.

He would speak to her in the morning before he and her brother, as arranged, would go speak to the deviant publisher. Devere, too, had insisted on accompanying them, and his presence couldn't hurt. It could not be denied that he was one of the most respected men in the Capital. And one of the wealthiest.

But even though Charles was not nearly as wealthy as the Beresfords, he and he alone would offer the bribe to the unscrupulous Hammond.

Georgiana was, after all, his wife.

CHAPTER EIGHT

WHEN SHE AWAKENED the morning after her wedding, Georgiana tiptoed into her dressing room and contrived to dress herself in a pale green dress she knew was becoming on her. Dressing her hair into a semblance of something attractive was even more of a challenge for one unaccustomed to such an effort. To compensate, she brushed it back and held it in place with generously applied pearl pins that had belonged to her mother. She peered into the looking glass above her dressing table, turning her head first to the right, then the left, satisfying herself that her appearance was acceptable.

Next, she tiptoed to the door that connected her dressing room with her husband's and slowly eased it open. Relief swished through her when she saw that he slept in his own bed at his own house. She stood there for several moments, savoring this small thrill of possession. *This is my husband.* Everything about him from his bare, muscled shoulders to his soft snores reeked of blatant masculinity.

She'd gone off to sleep the previous night, morose at the fear he was actually in the arms of his ladybird lover. The last time she had looked at the clock before drifting off to sleep, it was midnight. What time had he eventually come home? Had he left his lover's bed in order to face his wife the following morning?

The very thought cast a dark cloud over what should have

been the happiest time of her life: her wedding.

Quietly closing the door behind her, she went to the little desk that had belonged to his mother. One of her first duties as the new Lady Churston would be to order stationery with her new name and her husband's family's crest.

Thinking of a crest reminded her of the beautiful woman who looked like the late Mrs. Powell. How Georgiana wished she had paid better attention to the crest on the carriage that woman entered. To satisfy her own curiosity, Georgiana would love to know who the lady was.

She began penning a letter to her cousin, Lady Mary, who was temporarily living in Vienna with her diplomat husband. She knew Mary would share it with her sister, Lady Sophia Birmingham, who also lived in Vienna. Next time, Georgiana would write to Sophia, who would share her cousin's letter with Mary.

Several moments later, the opening of a door into her dressing room alerted her that Charles must have awakened. This sent a fluttering to her chest.

When he opened the door to her chamber, she looked up and smiled at him. In a short time, he had managed to dress himself suitably for paying morning calls and had even shaved himself. He had never held more appeal.

"You look lovely this morning, my dear."

Would her pulse always race when he referred to her as *my dear*? "And you, sir, have proven your skill at shaving yourself. I commend you. You look fit for Parliament."

"I suppose you're anxious to know what occurred last night."

"Very much so." Though she really didn't believe much could have been accomplished before the *Gazette* offices opened this morning.

"On Devere's advice, we met with John Murray."

"The publisher?"

"Yes. We merely picked his brain."

"He knows the *Gazette* publisher?"

"Only his unsavory reputation." Charles proceeded to tell her all he had learned the previous night.

"Please say that you're not going to offer to pay that horrid man to print a retraction!"

He shrugged. "I don't know what else I can do." He moved closer to the desk where she sat and gentled his voice. "I'd do anything to make you happy."

Her heart sang. "I hate to see his dishonesty line his pockets. Why can we not just sue him for libel?"

"Because that could take years. We need to stop this now."

"You're right, dearest."

He cupped his hand over hers. "I owe you a game a chess."

"Indeed you do."

"For now, we need to break the fast. I'll wager Cook has prepared us suitable fare."

They held hands as they descended the stairs to the modest morning room where the cook had set up offerings on a small sideboard. Georgiana poured tea for both of them, placed a muffin, a dollop of marmalade, and a baked egg on her plate, and then took a seat at a small table she suspected doubled as a game table.

"And how, my dear husband, do you take your tea?" she asked when he sat across the table from her. She wanted to know everything about this man she'd married.

"Lots of sugar and cream as well."

"Ah, my husband has a sweet tooth!"

"I do, indeed."

She prepared his tea and handed it to him. She was grateful for this opportunity to get to know him better. "How long has Cook been with you?" It only now occurred to her she hadn't met his cook.

He shrugged. "She's the niece of the cook who's served our family my entire life—and still serves my parents. I suppose my cook's been here for nearly ten years."

"Then she'll know all your favorite dishes?"

"I've tried to simplify things for her, seeing as I don't entertain at all. I've only had her do simple fare, but she's well aware of my preference for sweets and always manages to be baking something I eat ravenously."

She halved her muffin and pressed marmalade onto it. "Now that you're married, should you wish to entertain? Perhaps a dinner with some fellow Whigs and their wives?"

"I've never thought about it, but it does sound like something I would enjoy. My father would be ecstatic if I were more active in politics. And I might have some inclination toward it. Now that I'm married. I'll never measure up to your cousin Lady Harriett's husband, Lord Rockingham."

"Why do you say that?"

"The man is a paragon. He's well-liked, noble, honest, and he lives and breathes politics. Everyone says when the Whigs return to power, he will lead the country."

"Then it's very good he's family. You'll be an asset to him."

"I do plan to devote more time to such endeavors now that I'm a family man."

Her breathing quickened at the thought of Charles and her starting a family. She might be young, but she knew herself well, and she knew nothing could make her happier than having a family with this man and helping his political career in any way she could.

When she saw that he'd drained his delicate cup, she asked, "More tea?"

He handed the cup to her. "Please."

"Tell me some things you'd like to have for dinner. I plan to meet with Cook and work on upcoming menus."

He bestowed a wide smile on her. "I believe I'm going to enjoy being married. It will be nice to have my culinary whims answered. You can select the small dishes. All I care for is what comes from animals. Fish. Fowl. Lamb. Beef. Lots of meat, and I'm a happy man."

A smile lifted her face. "I, too, believe I'm going to enjoy being married."

"I'm told all maidens want nothing more than being married and running their own households. Is that true?"

"I cannot speak for all maidens. I do know that most women will not countenance a marriage for marriage's sake. Take my beautiful cousin Sophia."

"The one who married the youngest Birmingham brother?"

"Yes. She turned down seven-and-forty proposals of marriage. Poor Devere despaired his sister would never marry. But Lady Sophia knows her mind. She would not accept a man—no matter how titled or how wealthy—whom she did not love. When she met the man of her dreams, she knew it immediately."

Charles chuckled. "And he turned out to be one of the richest men in all of Europe."

"And he's handsome, too," she added with a smile.

"So you're quite close with your Beresford cousins?"

"Very. Our fathers were but a year apart, and they were close, almost like twins. We spent much of our childhoods going back and forth from Tilford to Hamberley. Hamberly was like a second home. I'm particularly close to Lady Harriett, as we're almost the same age. We both idolized Sophia. Did you know her?"

"By sight. A dark-haired beauty. All the Beresfords females are beautiful."

Except for Lucy, but Georgiana would never say that. She loved her sister too much. Besides, there was something about Lucy that captivated Lord Montague, and Georgiana understood that. Lucy was a lovely person. And with her physical frailty, she brought out a man's protective nature.

Georgiana supposed Charles felt protective toward her now because of the way that horrible newspaper persecuted her. Charles was a good man. That she inherently knew.

"Thank you. I always wished my hair were a darker brown, like Sophia's."

"Yours is perfect. You're perfect."

She could feel heat rushing to her face. "You're very kind."

"Kindness has nothing to do with it."

His gaze swept over her, making her feel even more self-conscious, especially when a deep blush colored her face.

"My sister Emily is often taken for my twin. There's only a year between us. You may have noticed at our wedding that she's a wee bit taller than me and perhaps a wee bit slenderer."

"I will own, I was rather taken with how similar you two look. Her hair's the same shade of medium brown as yours, and she has your dimples. It *was* a bit like seeing your twin." His voice lowered, and she thought he might be peering at her bosom. "You're prettier. You've got more curves."

Her face became even more heated.

He scooped the last bite of his second baked egg into his mouth and stood. "I'm shoving off now to meet Devere and James, who've insisted upon accompanying me to the *Gazette* office. You have my word I'll return here as soon as we're finished. We will play that game of chess."

LOCATED JUST OFF Fleet Street within throwing distance of St. Paul's, the *Gazette* occupied what appeared to be several former storefronts. On one side of the central door, printing presses were churning, and typesetters were busy lining up small blocks of type. On the other side, where they entered, a number of men scribbled behind desks.

Charles strode up to a clerk seated near the outer door. "Lord Devere, Lord Churston, and Mr. Beresford need to see Mr. Hammond," he said.

"Allow me to see if Mr. Hammond is in." The youthful, bespectacled clerk walked to the rear wall, opened a door, and disappeared down a dimly lit corridor.

Of course the fellow would know if his employer was in. The clerk obviously served as a screen.

A moment later, he returned. "I will show you to Mr. Hammond's office."

Charles didn't know what he had expected, but the small, cramped office spilling over with pamphlets, stacks of newspapers, and several towers of manuscripts was not it. Even the man himself did not bear any resemblance to how Charles thought a publisher ought to look. Hugh Hammond could not have looked more unlike the well-dressed John Murray.

Hammond's clothing looked as if he'd worn it for a decade without thought of cleaning. His cravat may once have been white, but it was now the color of sand and as limp as a wet newspaper. Charles judged the ruddily complected man's age to be fifty.

Hammond held out his hand. The fellow looked so filthy, Charles hated to touch it, but good manners prevailed—though this man did not deserve civility. Charles went on to perform the introductions.

"Do sit down, gents." Though his voice was not that of a gentleman, Hammond's speech was somewhere between that of the lower classes and that of an educated man. "You're not the only aristocrats who come to the offices of 'ugh 'ammond. I've got friends even loftier than yerselves."

The publisher's gaze, like a tiger sizing up its prey, went from Charles to James to Devere. "I believe I know why you important men are here today."

"You've been publishing libelous reports about an innocent woman," Charles said.

"We're powerful men, Hammond. You've picked on the wrong family," Devere added.

Hammond smirked. "Proving libel is difficult. I 'ave a person of exalted rank who's supplied me with information about your kinswoman. I choose to believe this person of exalted rank. Who's to say your Miss Beresford—who I believe is now Lady Churston—is not guilty of the things the *Gazette* has printed?"

Charles jumped up. Only by the greatest restraint did he quell his desire to crash a fist into the publisher's smug face. If he had been the butt of the *Gazette's* slurs, he wouldn't have hesitated to give the lying man a thorough trouncing. But he had Georgiana to consider.

"All of us are! It's a complete pack of lies, and we demand you retract every bit of it," Charles said.

His eyes cold as agate, Hammond shook his head. "That I refuse to do."

"I'm a very wealthy man," James said. "What's your price?"

Charles felt it was his obligation to incur the expense, but he did not want to argue about it here and now.

"There is no amount of money that will induce me to retract those articles. I stand by my source."

"We have no choice but to believe that source of yours—that person of exalted rank—has already well compensated you," Charles said. "I commend your loyalty." The filthy cur.

Devere stood, and then James followed. "We will be proceeding with a libel suit."

"You know that can take years," Hammond said.

"We would have preferred to handle this matter today," Charles said. "But you've turned down the opportunity to become a very rich man."

Hammond's eyes sparkled with mischief. "Ah, but I'm already a very wealthy man. All my needs are met. As I said, I have influential friends in high places."

Not friends. Puppet masters.

BEFORE CHARLES WENT home to share the disappointing news with his wife, he went to see his family's lawyer and initiated steps to file a libel suit against Hugh Hammond and his *Gazette*.

Between his lawyer's establishment in the city and his home in Mayfair, Charles dreaded telling Georgiana he'd failed her.

Even more, he hated that he was powerless to lift her gloom, to restore her good name.

He thought, too, about who the powerful person of such exalted rank could be. That person, for reasons unknown to him or the Beresfords, wanted to destroy Georgiana. How could that be? She'd only been in London two days when the first attack upon her appeared in the *Gazette*. Before that, she hadn't been in London in over a year.

As much as he did not want to distress her, they needed to explore these attacks further. He meant to find out if there was a spurned lover who was retaliating against her.

CHAPTER NINE

W HEN GEORGIANA'S HUSBAND arrived at their house, her sisters, Lady Montague and Emily Beresford, were leaving. "We couldn't persuade your wife to join us," Lady Montague said. "The newlywed could not bear to be absent when her husband returned."

His smiling gaze shifted from her sister to his bride. "What a nice reception I've come home to." He moved to Georgiana and brushed his lips against her smooth cheek. "Thank you for choosing me over your lovely sisters."

After her sisters left, he led her to the library where they sat on a velvet sofa in front of the fire. He took her hand, held it between both his, and met her solemn gaze with one equally as solemn.

"You had no success," she said.

He nodded. "We tried our best, but the man was unmovable. He claims someone of an exalted rank supplied him with the information, and that person, to him, is unimpeachable."

Her voice forlorn, she said, "I have no enemies. I know of no one who hates me and especially no one who could hate me that much."

He brought her hand to his lips. "This sounds like the evildo-ings of a spurned lover. When you came out last year, you must have broken some man's heart irrevocably."

"I can't believe that."

He gave her a skeptical look. "I find it difficult to believe you didn't turn down a single offer."

"Oh, I didn't say that."

"Then you did turn down an offer of marriage?"

She nodded.

"Just one rejection?"

"No."

"How many rejections, Georgiana?"

She didn't think Charles had ever referred to her by her Christian name before. The intimacy of it gladdened her. She mumbled former suitors' names under her breath as fingers calculated. "Five."

"It's my good fortune you turned them down."

That comment, too, gladdened her. "No, it's my good fortune. Do not allow your chest to swell when I tell you you're infinitely superior to those men."

He tossed his head back and chuckled. "I reiterate. I am a fortunate man. I do believe the only thing that explains your recent persecution must be coming from one of those five men. Did any of the men strike you as being vindicative?"

"No. I believe they took my rejection in good stride. They were perfectly behaved gentlemen. I can't believe any of them could ever be so cruel." She shrugged. "And in all honesty, I don't believe any of them possessed violent feelings toward me."

"Ah, but you know not your allure, my lady."

It was still difficult to believe she was being addressed as *my lady*. Her first inclination was to say he was being kind, but he'd already objected to that. "Thank you for the unmerited praise, my dearest."

His gold-flecked eyes flashed with mirth. "You know I'm going to assure you such praise is merited."

"Then you, sir, must know I going to say you're too kind."

"I'm not kind. In fact, I'm wishing to do murder to one of your former suitors. Will you share their names with me?"

"I am told married people are to share everything with one another."

"That's a good way to start a marriage. I'll begin by pledging to always be honest with you."

"And I will do the same with you."

"Then we're getting off to a proper start."

Proper, but not complete. She wouldn't feel truly married until she had given herself completely to him. Her husband.

"I will tell you the names, but I cannot believe any of those men could be responsible for the meanness behind the *Gazette's* lies."

"Perhaps I may know something detrimental about one of them that you do not."

She held out an index finger. "The first one was a viscount, Lord Aldridge."

"Ah, he's my age. A good man."

She nodded.

"I know nothing unfavorable about him. We were at Eton together. And the second?"

"Stewart Cunningham."

He screwed up his face. "I don't believe I know him."

"Of course, you wouldn't. He's not in Parliament, and he's quite old. Close to forty, I'd say."

"I'll see what I can learn about him."

"The third man was so very nice I could never believe anything uncivil about him."

"And who would that be?"

"The Marquess of Straeham."

His brows wiggled. "Many women would consider him quite a conquest."

She wrinkled her nose. "The man was older than my late Papa."

"There is that. I suppose he was seeking a mother for his large brood."

"I think you're right. It's wicked of me, but I'd prefer raising children of my own."

He gave her what could only be described as a seductive, heavy-lidded gaze. "I shall look forward to that."

Her heart soared. Dare she concur? She mustn't seem too eager. "In time, dearest. It will make me happy, too." At least she hadn't admitted to how much she craved a union with this man. What woman wouldn't want children of her own?

"And your next spurned suitor?" he asked.

"That would be Sir Thomas Ely."

"I do know him." Charles's eyes narrowed with what could only be construed as displeasure.

"You find him objectionable?"

"Turning him down was a wise decision. Who's the last man?"

"James's best friend, whom I've known all my life and who, I assure you—and my brother would assure you—is a very well-respected man."

"Turning him down must have been difficult."

"It was one of the hardest things I've ever done because I've always been so fond of him. I didn't want to hurt him."

"Why did you not desire to marry him?"

"It wouldn't have been fair to marry a man I wasn't in love with."

He then smiled at her. "Enough of this unpleasantness. I'll set up the chessboard. I did promise my wife a game."

GEORGIANA HAD PROVEN to be a far more skilled chess player than she'd admitted. They had then dined on one of the most satisfactory dinners he'd had in many weeks. His wife was to be commended for it. She had encouraged Cook to prepare an abundance of fish, fowl, and beef. Yes, he was going to enjoy being married. Especially to Georgiana.

After dinner, he was able to collect Freddie from his lodgings at Albany before heading to Brook's on St. James. They would start at Brook's, since that's where they spent most of their evenings. Later, he might go to White's.

Charles felt badly that he'd left his wife alone again on just the second night of their marriage. But he and Freddie needed to discuss Sir Thomas. And perhaps her other former suitors. The sooner he discovered who was behind this torment of his wife, the better.

When they first arrived at Brook's, he and Freddie sat alone at one of the small tables, and Charles apprised his friend of his suspicions that a spurned suitor of his wife's might be behind the attacks on her.

"So you know who these men are?" asked Freddie.

Charles enumerated them.

"Can't believe anything unfavorable about Aldridge."

"Nor can I."

"And Lord Straeham's widely respected."

"I agree."

Freddie's nose wrinkled. "That Sir Thomas is a nasty one!" Freddie said.

"It fairly makes my blood curdle to even contemplate that man with Georgiana."

"To her credit, she knew better than to trust the blighter."

Charles thought of what the *Gazette* publisher had said about his source. "Would you ever refer to Sir Thomas as one of exalted rank?"

"Never! Fellow's always got pockets to let."

Had the man been in love with Georgiana, or was he interested in her dowry? Charles could not understand how every bachelor in the Capital could not have wanted to marry his beautiful Georgiana. "That's what I thought." He told Freddie about his fruitless visit to speak to the *Gazette* publisher.

"But that scoundrel Sir Thomas would as soon lie as breathe. Never knew him to tell the truth."

"He's a thoroughly disreputable character. Haven't seen him in an age."

"Remember he was blackballed from White's when he was caught cheating. Was it at Faro?"

Charles shrugged. "I only remember the cheating part. I remember, too, that he was also blocked from gaining membership to Brook's."

Freddie's brows drew together. "Despicable man. On so many levels. Can't abide a fellow who brags about his conquests with other fellows' wives, either."

"He does seem to measure women by what he can get from them." Thank God Georgiana had the good sense to turn him down. Charles could not imagine anything more unequal—or disgusting—than a union between the swine and the innocent Georgiana.

"Don't know what you could learn by talking to the vile fellow. Can't see him here or at White's. Where is the man received?"

"I'm guessing he's not been blackballed by Almack's. It's my assumption my wife may have met him there when she came out last year."

"It's understandable those patronesses likely wouldn't know what a blighter he is. It's not like men go about gossiping like women."

"True." Not even to Georgiana had he thought of repeating all the disreputable things he knew about Sir Thomas.

"If you tried to question him, he'd only lie," Freddie said.

Charles knew his friend was right. "We seem to know a lot about a man we've never been friends with."

"Because of the trail of ill repute he leaves in his wake."

"Ill repute does describe him."

"But my sister tells me women find him handsome and are attracted to him," Freddie said.

Charles pictured the man. He was perhaps three or four years older than Charles and was possessed of black hair, very white skin, and startling blue eyes. Added to his so-called attractiveness to women was his taller-than-average height and a body that lent credit to his tailor's creations.

"We've been confining our suspicions to the likely culprit, but we ought to discuss the others. Do you know Stewart Cunningham? My wife believes him to be nearing forty years of age."

Freddie pursed his lips as he contemplated the question. He then shook his head. "Must not be a member of Brook's. We could ask some members here if they know him."

"How will you explain such questioning?"

"Can always say I owe the fellow money."

"That ought to merit a helpful response." It bothered Charles that if the man were to be sitting right in front of them, neither he nor Freddie would know him. Fortunately, he believed they knew everyone at Brook's.

Freddy swigged at his brandy, pushed away from the table, and said, "I'm off to discover what I can about this Cunningham. Why do you not make inquiries about the disreputable Sir Thomas?"

"It couldn't hurt."

While Freddie moved from table to table in the front chamber, Charles went into the rear room and, using the pretext that Sir Thomas owed him a large sum of money, went to each table and explained why he was looking for Sir Thomas and asking if anyone knew where to find him.

None of his acquaintances knew where to find the scoundrel, but to a man, they all scowled at the mention of his name.

This made Charles believe that Devere or James might have enlightened Georgiana on the character of the sinister man who sought her hand in marriage. Had he a sister, Charles would have forbidden any association with one as unscrupulous as Sir Thomas Ely.

Next, Charles climbed the stairs and made inquiries among the men gathered there. There, Albert Marshall said, "You'll never get back a penny from him, but I believe you can find him lodging in Bloomsbury at one Mrs. Hancock's establishment." Marshall shook his head. "I wouldn't have thought you'd ever been foolish enough, Churston, to loan that scoundrel money."

"It was the most foolish thing I've ever done." Thankfully, he wasn't that stupid. "I appreciate the information, Marshall."

When he and Freddie returned to their table, Freddie told him he only found one man who knew Cunningham. "Fellow is said to be wealthy. Comes from a long line of prosperous farmers and owns a large chunk of Sussex. Has a Whitehall mansion. Not noble but said to be a gentleman."

"I found out where Sir Thomas lives."

"Think we should pay them calls?"

"Yes, but allow me to think on it. I haven't yet decided what I'm going to say."

Charles left Freddie playing Faro at Brook's. For the next hour, he rode around London, thinking of just how he would approach these men. What could he do to discover if either of them were responsible for the lies printed about his wife?

As badly as he wanted to blame Sir Thomas, Charles's gut told him Sir Thomas was not capable of orchestrating such a slur against Georgiana. Not because he could possibly possess a noble character, but because the man did not fit with what the unscrupulous publisher had told them about the person supplying the false information. The person responsible for the attacks on his wife was of *exalted* rank. Charles was fairly certain that let out Sir Thomas and Cunningham. The liar also had to be possessed of a vast fortune. Which also let out Sir Thomas.

As dishonest as the publisher was, Charles believed the disreputable Hammond answered to a person of deep pockets and high rank. Neither of these men matched that description.

Still, Charles needed to speak to the men himself. Perhaps he'd been able to uncover something useful to aid his quest.

CHAPTER TEN

T WO NIGHTS IN a row—the first two nights of their marriage—her bridegroom had left her alone. Tonight he'd said
he and Freddie Fortescue were going to learn what they could
about her rejected suitors.

Had he told her the truth? Was he really going to the arms of
his ladybird? Just today he had vowed he would always tell her
the truth. But no man would tell his wife about his mistress. It
wasn't done.

In spite of her upsetting doubts, she was inclined to believe
her husband. She had always been a good judge of character. She
had been the only girl at her school in Devon who had suspected
a popular fellow student was being led astray. She'd neither seen
nor heard anything to prove her suspicions about the girl. It was
just a strong feeling based on her knowledge of human nature.
She had known the girl was hiding something. Everyone except
Georgiana was shocked when it was revealed that the handsome
gardener had gotten the girl in a family way.

With this same conviction, Georgiana knew Charles was a
good man. If he told her he wouldn't lie to her, she would believe
him.

But why in the devil was she so worried another woman had
won his affections before he'd ever met her?

How long would it take him and Freddie to learn about her

former suitors? Would Charles attempt to speak to any of them tonight?

She finished the letter to her cousin Mary in Vienna, reread Rousseau until she could no longer keep her eyelids open, and once more went to her bedchamber to sleep alone.

SINCE IT WAS night—and fairly late now—Charles knew Sir Thomas would not be at home. That type of man slept all day and prowled at night. Hopefully, though, Charles might be able to catch Mr. Cunningham at home.

Charles felt guilty for throwing out his aristocratic card to gain admittance to the man's fine mansion at this time of night, but he'd always found that those not born to peers' families were flattered by their attentions.

Moment after arriving at Cunningham's doorstep, his footman said, "Mr. Cunningham will see you in his library." Charles was then led down a corridor inlaid with a mixture of sienna, black, and white marble. Everything about the house from the gilded mirrors and matching sconces to the glittering, multi-tiered crystal chandelier which illuminated the spiral staircase bespoke impeccable taste and uncommon wealth.

This excellent taste extended to the library with its dark walnut wood, jewel-colored tomes lining the shelves, and the crimson velvet draperies and plush sofas. Charles took a seat in front of the fireplace, where the fire had begun to smolder. Obviously, the home's owner had not expected company at this time of night.

That man, who was at least a dozen years older than Charles, entered the chamber and offered Charles a warm greeting. "Ah, the fortunate man who's won Miss Beresford's hand," he said.

Charles observed that the fellow was not unattractive. He was nearly as tall as Charles, well-built, and in possession of a thick head of dark blond hair. "Forgive the lateness of the hour," Charles said as he shook the man's proffered hand. "I'm here because of the horrible lies the *Gazette* has printed about my wife."

"Please sit down." Mr. Cunningham indicated the sofa where Charles had been sitting, and he came to sit next to him. "I don't believe I've ever read the *Gazette*. I am unaware of the attacks to which you refer. And forgive my bluntness, but I fail to understand why you've wanted this audience with me."

"You have every right to wonder. My wife has explained that last year you sought her hand in marriage."

"That's true. She's a lovely woman, and I won't deny I envy you."

"She speaks highly of you. I am desperate to learn who is using the *Gazette* to print unspeakable lies about her. You must know she's incapable of immorality."

"Of course! I think that innocent quality about her was every bit as enticing as her beauty."

"Can you think of anyone who might be responsible for these assaults to her character?"

Cunningham shook his head. "The most likely explanation would be a spurned lover, but I assure you, that man is not me. In fact, I only recently married. Happily. I have no rancor toward the former Miss Beresford. Another possibility only just this moment occurred to me. Could a former lover of yours resent Miss Beresford so violently that she wished to disgrace her?"

"It's a clever thought, but there's been but one woman to whom I've ever showered my affections, and it's my good fortune to have married her."

"So you're theorizing that the responsible party must be one of your wife's spurned suitors?"

"Meaning no disrespect to you, sir, that's true." Even though it was possible this man could be manipulating him, and even though Cunningham was obviously wealthy enough to control the *Gazette*, Charles could not believe this thoughtful man could possibly be behind the attacks on Georgiana.

"I do remember that before I met Miss Beresford, one Sir Thomas Ely was exceedingly annoying in his attentions to her. Even after she refused him, he kept hanging about her cousin's house, trying to woo her, trying to force her to change her mind."

Charles nodded. "I'm aware of the man's unprincipled behavior, and I do plan to pursue that avenue of investigation." Charles stood. "I'm grateful to you for seeing me tonight."

Cunningham stood.

Charles's head inclined ever so slightly in a bow. "Felicitations on your marriage. I hope you and your fortunate bride have a long and happy life together."

"And the same to you, my lord."

FROM HER VACATED dressing chamber, Charles tapped at his wife's bedchamber door. Thorne had renewed his duties of assisting his master to shave and dress this morning, and Charles had heard Georgiana and her maid in the dressing room.

"Come in, dearest."

He strolled into her chamber. Seeing how lovely she looked in a simple sprigged muslin dress as she sat at his mother's former desk buoyed him with pride. It was still difficult to believe that this lovely creature was his very own wife. Instead of continuing to declare her beauty, this morning he simply walked up to her and brushed his lips across her flawless cheek. "Good morning to you, my love."

There was no smile for him this morning. Instead she queried him, her expression inscrutable. "What time did you return last night? It must have been quite late."

"It was late. I'll tell you everything. Will you allow me to ring and ask that we take breakfast in this chamber?" He preferred the intimate setting. She must have, too, for she agreed.

He lowered his tall frame onto the settee and asked her to come sit beside him in front of the fire. Moments later, their breakfast offerings were placed on a low table in front of them, and she poured his tea, preparing it exactly as he had requested yesterday.

He told her what he'd done the previous night. "It was wretched of me to barge in on Cunningham, but the fellow couldn't have been nicer."

"I told you that."

"And you were right. I cannot believe him capable of those attacks on you. Did you know he recently married?"

"No, but you'll recall I had just arrived back in the capital the day before you and I met on Piccadilly. When I'm home at Tilford Hall, I rarely read the London newspapers—except when they write about Parliament. I like to see what Devere's up to. And since Harriett's married Lord Rockingham, I now like to see what he's doing in the House of Commons."

"And now you'll have to read about your husband." He balanced his plate of baked eggs and muffins on his lap.

She finally smiled. "I shall look forward to it. And I'm glad you realize Mr. Cunningham is a dear soul. I'm sure he'll make a fine husband." She shrugged. "There was simply no . . . I don't know how to phrase it, but as much as I admire him, his presence didn't have that champagne effect upon me."

He knew what she meant. It couldn't be true love without a deep, elevating physical reaction to the person of the opposite sex. Some people called it a spark. He thought he preferred the *champagne effect*.

She certainly had that effect upon him. Just being this close to her—especially with her cozy bed just behind them—most definitely prompted a physical reaction in him. Not just in the hardening of a certain part of his anatomy. He longed to touch that flower-petal skin, to press against the soft curves of her, to kiss her with all his heart. Being with her was always sweet anguish.

He wanted to ask her if he possibly produced such a feeling in her, but he did not want to hear the answer if it were negative. Still, he consoled himself that he must appeal to her on some level, or else she wouldn't have consented to marry him. Should he tell her how she affected him? He feared he was too proud for his own good, but he would not permit himself to risk humiliation.

As he concentrated on cleaning his plate, he contemplated telling her how she ignited his spark, but by the time his food was gone, he still hadn't gathered the courage to tell her.

When she was finished eating, he put his empty plate back on the table, took his last sip of now-cool tea, and then he settled back and settled his arm around her shoulders. This resulted in her leaning into him. He was powerless not to press a kiss on her temple.

She settled her splayed hand on his thigh, and he thought he could quite possibly go mad with want of her. Were her hand to move up a few more inches, she would discover the bulge he was mightily hoping she would not see.

He not only needed to distract her, he gravely needed a distraction. Otherwise he'd be craving to feel her hands on his swollen shaft . . . and craving all those other things that went along with his crippling hunger for her.

"What do you know of Sir Thomas's character?" he asked. *I must get my mind off this alluring woman.*

She did not answer for a moment. "I wasn't entirely honest when I said all my former suitors were gentlemen."

"Go on."

"I don't like to speak ill of anyone, but when Sir Thomas first called on me, Devere told me in private to avoid the man at all costs. According to my cousin, Sir Thomas is a scoundrel."

"Your cousin is to be commended for apprising you of the truth about the man. I, too, dislike speaking negatively about anyone, but in this case, it's warranted. I presume you took Devere's advice?"

"Of course. I respect him and know he was trying to protect me. I cannot deny that I was initially attracted to Sir Thomas. He's quite handsome. But I found out soon enough that he's not a gentleman. The man could not accept rejection. He rather stalked me. It got to where I hid when I saw him, to where I told all the servants that if he called, I was not in. I finally returned to Tilford just to rid myself of the man's presence, but I still feared he would come after me to Lincolnshire." She looked up at him. "Do you think the wretched man could be responsible for the *Gazette*'s lies about me? Could he resent me that much?"

"While he could very well have instigated these attacks—and there's nothing I wouldn't believe him capable of—I have difficulty believing him guilty."

"Why?"

"Because I'm almost certain the person the unscrupulous publisher answers to is extremely wealthy."

She nodded. "And Sir Thomas has no money. It pains me to admit the man had set his sights on my dowry, not me."

Charles lifted her hand to his mouth, flipped it to put her palm up, then pressed a kiss into the cup of her palm. Flame climbed into her cheeks. Their eyes met and held, then her lashes lowered. She swallowed, and he grew even harder. His tender action had certainly affected her.

When her hand went back to settle intimately on his thigh, he suppressed a groan. *She's such an innocent, she doesn't realize how thoroughly she's tormenting me.* "Be assured, my dear, I'd have wed you if you had no dowry."

"Thank you, dearest. Do I get you today for a rematch of our chess game?" she asked wistfully.

"There's nothing I'd like more," he said, knowing as soon as he'd said it, there was indeed something else he'd rather do with her, "but I have to go to the House of Commons today." He stood, positioning himself behind the back of the settee so she would not see how she'd physically affected him. "I don't like leaving you, but why do you not see to the redecoration of this chamber today? Engage the painters and drapers, whatever you need."

"I'd almost forgotten. I shall enjoy that."

"I promise to have dinner with you tonight."

"Could we eat once more in this chamber?"

"Whatever my wife wants." *God give me strength.*

CHAPTER ELEVEN

THE AGED, LAUGHINGSTOCK Lord Swinnerton had just taken the floor and was launching into one of his hours-long pleas to strike peers from taxation. Charles could think of no better time to exit. It was also a good time to try to catch that swine, Sir Thomas, at home.

When Charles came out of the Palace of Westminster, the sun had almost disappeared as dusk darkened daylight. He drove his phaeton to Bloomsbury but had no notion of where Mrs. Hancock's establishment was. He managed to stop a hackney driver and ask. The surprisingly well-spoken driver gave Charles clear instructions on how to reach the house where Sir Thomas stayed. It helped that it was on one of the borough's main streets.

He easily found the house. Houses in this respectable section of Bloomsbury, while not grand, were well kept. Beyond Mrs. Hancock's shiny black door, a vestibule area displayed a printed directory of the residents. Sir Thomas Wilcox resided at number 200.

Charles mounted the wooden staircase and discovered that 200 comprised an entire floor of the four-story house. Apparently, Mrs. Hancock had been impressed by her lodger's title. Charles wondered how far in arrears Sir Thomas was and could not help but feel sympathy for the poor, duped landlady who thought she would be hosting a fine gentleman.

When Charles tapped at Sir Thomas's door, he was surprised the man actually answered the door himself. Had the man lost all his servants for failure to pay their salaries?

Though he was not a judge of handsomeness in men, Charles's quick appraisal of the fellow told him the scoundrel was blessed with good looks. His build was certainly favorable, and the fellow's height was considerably above average. There was nothing offensive about his face, and his black hair was styled fashionably. Sir Thomas's black brows rose in query.

Charles handed him his card. "Might I have a word?"

"Of course, my lord." Sir Thomas, still dressed in afternoon attire, held open his door for Charles to enter the messy parlor. Charles's own messes consisted of stacks of yellowing newspapers he was reluctant to throw out. But, as newspapers were expensive, there were no newspapers in Sir Thomas's parlor. Only the odd half-finished cup of tea, an assortment of plates and glasses with bits of food and drink, and coats slung across the backs of chairs littered this man's living quarters.

"Forgive the disarray," Sir Thomas said. "My servant has left because of a family emergency, and I'm hopeless at these things. You know how it is."

Looking past the untidiness, the chamber was decently furnished with a mock velvet sofa and two sturdy armchairs.

"I'm rather hopeless myself when I lose the services of my man."

"Won't you have a seat?"

"I prefer to stand. What I've come to speak to you about won't take long. Two days ago it was my good fortune to marry Miss Georgiana Beresford."

Sir Thomas ran a swift, appraising gaze over his visitor. "You are to be commended. She's a lovely girl."

"Thank you." Charles drew a long breath. "During the past week, my poor wife has been the victim of slanderous, untrue assaults on her character in the *Gazette*. Someone is trying to destroy her. I believe it must be someone seeking vengeance."

Sir Thomas froze. Then, eyes narrowed, he spoke in a hardened voice. "You think I'm vindictive toward her because she turned down my offer of marriage?"

"It's merely a possibility I'm exploring."

"Well, you can strike me off your list! Yes, I was crushed when she rejected me. I even tried my mightiest to get her to change her mind. But crushing women with cruelty is not one of my sins. And I won't deny I've many sins. What I felt for her was genuine—and still is."

This Charles could understand. The man was still in love with Georgiana. Charles was inclined to believe him. "Have you any idea who could be behind these attacks on her?"

"To be truthful, this sounds like the work of a woman."

Charles pondered the statement a moment, chiding himself for not thinking of it. "I'd never considered that possibility, but you could be right."

"If the instigator should prove to be a man," Sir Thomas said, "I could kill him myself. You see, Churston, I do have my sins."

"I'm sorry if I misjudged you." Charles held out his hand as a peace offering. "Thank you for your time—and for the suggestion." He started for the door, then turned back. "I, too, could kill the man who would do this to my wife." *My wife.* Nothing had ever filled him with more pride than uttering those words.

⇻⇺

OVER A COZY dinner in her chamber, Georgiana's husband told her about the meeting with Sir Thomas.

"See, he's not a wicked man," she defended.

"Oh, he's wicked enough. I just don't believe he is toward you. Apparently, he's still in love with you."

"I doubt that. I didn't spend enough time with him to have cultivated that kind of devotion."

"You don't believe in such a thing as love at first sight?" he asked.

She couldn't answer for a moment. The question had hit far too close to home. She not only believed in love at first sight, she had experienced it. It was just as real and as blazing as that fire in front of them—minus the probability of dying out. This love, she knew, would never die.

Though she could acknowledge love at first sight to herself, she couldn't to him. She made a non-committal response. "I'm not denying its existence."

His face inscrutable, her husband nodded. "Sir Thomas did say something worth exploring."

"What?" she asked.

"He said such an attack sounds like something a woman would do. I'm inclined to believe that's a possibility."

She had never thought of such a thing, but gossipy threats were behavior that was more indicative of a female. "I suppose Sir Thomas is cleverer than we realized. The lies printed in the *Gazette* do sound like the work of a woman. There's just one problem with that theory."

"What?"

"I know of no woman who would wish me harm. As with the men, I have no enemies."

"Come, come, my dear. A beautiful woman like you is bound to summon jealousy in other women. Perhaps a woman blames you for stealing away her lover. How do you know one of those five men who offered you marriage was not loved by a woman of violent jealousies?"

She was stunned. Though thrilled to hear him praise her beauty, she had difficulty believing any woman could hold so much malice toward her she would spread such vicious lies in the press. "But you forget I've been gone from London for almost a year now," she said. "Any rancor I might have drawn from a jealous woman last Season would have mellowed away in a year's time. Such a spurned woman may even have won back the affections of a man who may have been attracted to me."

"I admit the time lapse does weaken this theory."

"But who's to say the woman isn't one whose affections *you* spurned?"

"You can disavow yourself of that notion. You yourself said I've spent my time away from London's ballrooms in the *manly pursuits*."

"You never were in love?"

"Never."

She hoped he could fall in love with her.

"Tell me," he began, "who all knew you were back in London? Didn't you say you'd just arrived two days before the *Gazette's* first attack?"

"Actually, if one counts the night of my arrival, I arrived three days before the *Gazette's* lies appeared. Then the day before—which was my second whole day in London—was the day of my clumsiness on Piccadilly. Which resulted in our . . . meeting."

"You weren't clumsy."

"Oh, but I am. I should have warned you of my history." She gave a mock scowl. "My whole family despairs of my propensity to fall. A lot. James sometimes calls me Roly Poly."

"I do hope there's nothing wrong with you."

"Oh, I'm fit as a fiddle. I just tend to act too impetuously. Often."

He gave her an amused, good-natured smile. "Like in consenting to marry a virtual stranger?"

"That was rather impetuous. But I don't think it was horribly risky. I keenly felt that you were a good man, and you've done nothing since to destroy my confidence in you." No man could have been more concerned about her or more kind to her. For now, that would have to be enough.

"I would like to be worthy of your trust. Now, tell me who—other than members of your family—knew you'd arrived in London."

She sipped her wine and thought back. "No one other than family members. I suppose my sister or one of my cousins could have mentioned to someone that I was coming."

"Ask."

"I'll talk to them tomorrow—when my husband is off serving in Parliament." She shook her head. "My sister and Caroline Devere have just found out about the second attack on me in the *Gazette*, and they're very upset."

He cupped his hand over hers. The gesture warmed her from the tips of her toes to the tendrils of her stylishly arranged hair. "Let's discuss something happier. Did you make any progress today with the decorating of this chamber?"

"I did. My sister and I went to the linen drapers and selected a lovely silk and complementary velvet." She wouldn't tell him how she'd been stared at by the other patrons. Nor would she tell him how she'd heard her name mumbled by women who had obviously read the lies that had been printed about her in the *Gazette*. Since he was already expending so much of his own time trying to extricate her from this horrid unpleasantness, she did not want to add to his woes.

Moreover, she didn't want him to be ashamed of her or regret marrying a scandalous woman.

"Good," he said. "You went with pink?"

"I did."

"And what of the painters?"

She forced a smile. "I'm next on their list. They might be able to start tomorrow."

He kissed her hand and returned his attention to eating the last two bites of mutton. Then he looked at the untouched mutton on her plate. "Are you finished?"

She giggled. "I am. Do you wish to finish mine, too?"

"Of course. I told you I'm a ravenous meat eater."

"And sweet eater."

He took her plate. "That's why I'm so sweet."

She enjoyed every moment in this man's company. He had a gift for taking her mind off unpleasantries. He might not be in love with her, but she had no doubts that he cared about her and not just in the way one cares about a stranger who's fallen on hard times. Her husband gave every indication he cared deeply for her. "It's no joking matter. You are sweet. I'm fortunate to have you for my husband."

He set both plates on the table. "And I'm the lucky fellow who won the hand of the beautiful Georgiana Beresford."

"Are you sure you have no regrets?"

He shook his head emphatically. "No regrets." He stood and looked down at her. "Shall we go to the library for that game of chess?"

⤛⤜

HE'D HAD TO get away from her bedchamber. He'd given her his word he wouldn't be taking liberties with her until the relationship between them had sufficient time to be nurtured. For him, that moment couldn't come too soon.

Though his knowledge of women was limited, he knew they didn't have the same sexual drives as men. Men could get it off with a woman who did not appeal to them. He'd been one of those men.

But no more. The thought of such intimacy with any woman other than his Georgiana repulsed him. And the thought of making love to her was driving him mad with nearly debilitating desire.

First and foremost, he must be mindful of her innocence. He mustn't rush the consummation of their marriage. It could be so shocking to a maiden that it could do irreparable harm to his hopes of a highly compatible love life in their future.

When would be the right time? He'd been telling himself he'd know when the time came. Hopefully, his sweet Georgiana would make some gesture to indicate she was ready.

He was thinking these things as he set up the chessboard in front of the library's fire, and he had no control over how profoundly those thoughts affected him physically. He cursed the life that sprang in his groin.

He looked down at her. She was staring at his bulge. And then she looked up at him. Their eyes locked. "You do want me," she murmured.

"You have no idea how much," he answered huskily.

She nodded solemnly. "Please take me to your bed."

CHAPTER TWELVE

A S THEY CLIMBED the stairs, connected by her trembling clutching of his hand, her heart pounded so loudly she wondered if he could hear. The solid touch of his hand awakened her even more to the depths of his virility.

He walked her first to her door. "I'll go and tell my man I won't need his services either tonight or in the morning." His head lowered, and his lips touched hers softly.

In her bedchamber, she rang for Peg to help her into her bedclothes. She wore that frilly white linen and lace night shift, the one she'd gotten with Charles in mind. Peg combed out her hair. "I will likely be in my husband's room in the morning, so I won't be needing you," she told her maid.

Then she went to Charles's chamber and stood in the doorway of her dressing room, looking into his connecting bedchamber. He stood there barefoot but dressed except for the coat and cravat he'd removed. His shimmering gaze ever so slowly sifted over her body.

She watched the place where men swelled before making love, and his huge erection exhilarated her.

He moved closer and drew her into his arms for a hungry, breathless kiss. Her mouth opened to greedily receive his tongue. It was as if her mouth were connected to that most intimate part of her, for she began to throb. Low.

She couldn't seem to get close enough to him. Her clothing felt like an iron barrier. She pressed harder and harder against his swollen member until his hands cupped her buttocks, starting a slow, lulling rhythm that built to a frenzy as she pressed even harder against him.

He finally pulled away. "I'll snuff the lamp."

Even after he turned off the oil lamp, the room was not in complete darkness because of the fire in his hearth. He tossed off his shirt and came to her, his bare skin golden in the firelight.

"Will you allow me to remove this?" His hands cupped her breasts as he bent to cover a nipple with his mouth, wetting the thin fabric. Her breasts, now heavy, connected with that place low in her torso, and a raging desire began to strum through her.

Her own need to become one with this man overtook even her ability to form a response. She merely nodded, and he slowly lifted off her night rail, trailing her flesh with moist, butterfly kisses.

She'd thought she would be mortified to be standing un-clothed in front of a man. But this was not just a man. This was her husband, the man she loved. In their wedding ceremony she had pledged to give him her body, and this she was now doing most willingly.

Even as his heavy-lidded gaze lingered at her breasts, then lower still at the thatch that covered that place that now dripped with liquid heat, she was not embarrassed. She was empowered.

He lifted her in his arms and laid her on the bed, then slipped off his breeches and settled on his belly beside her as they hungrily kissed. This lovemaking she'd been longing for brought her even closer to him than she'd thought possible. But as much as she enjoyed the kissing, she wanted more. She wanted to feel him inside her. Unconscious of what she was doing, her thighs parted.

His fingers glided into her. Her shock at this incredible inti-macy wasn't as great as her need. It felt too deliriously good. She rocked into the movement of his hand.

Soon, his rod replaced his fingers. This was it. This was what she had been hungering for.

That was her last cognizant thought as wave after wave of shudders overcame her, drenched her, fulfilled her. This is what it felt like to be possessed. This is what it felt like to become one with one's spouse. This is what she'd been craving since she'd fallen in love with Viscount Churston, her Charles, her husband.

How long it lasted, she was powerless to say. It would never have been long enough. Nothing had ever given her such pleasure.

When it was over and her husband lay beside her, his breathing labored, his beloved body slick with sweat, she knew he had enjoyed it as much as she.

It was only then, when the joy of their mating was waning, that she realized how sore she was. Would her body ever accommodate him without the pain? She realized, too, she was lying in her own maiden's blood.

⋙⋘

WHEN HE COULD trust his ragged voice to steady enough for speech, he propped himself up on one elbow and gazed into her beautiful face. She looked like one drugged. He couldn't believe this most precious being had wanted him as powerfully as he'd wanted her. He stroked the wet hair from her brow. "Thank you, my love, for the best night of my life."

Then he settled his lips tenderly on hers. "I know there was pain, but I've been told that goes away after a maiden's body becomes accustomed to a man."

He knew there would be blood. "Shall we move now to your bed? After a while, we could . . . make love again. If you have no objections."

She pulled his head back down. "No objections."

God, but he was going love being married to this woman.

>>>><<<<

WHEN SHE AWAKENED the next morning after a night of blissful lovemaking, she glowed—and not just from the morning sun peeking into her chamber. Even her complete nakedness did not cause embarrassment. There was no part of her body her husband's hands or mouth had not explored during their long night of shared passion. Once more, she recalled the words of their wedding ceremony. Her body was her husband's, his hers. Her gaze fell on his bare shoulders, and she was nearly overcome by this powerful sense of possession. *This man is mine.*

With every rise and fall of his muscled shoulders, she gloried in the fact she was truly his now, truly married. Her heartbeat thumped in gladness when it occurred to her that she could at this very moment be carrying his seed.

His eyes came open, and he smiled upon her. "Good morning, wife of mine."

She returned the smile. "Good morning to you."

He came up on his elbow and regarded her with concern. "How are you feeling?"

She knew he referred to the soreness between her thighs. "The good outweighs any discomfort."

He drew her into his arms and pressed gentle kisses into her temple. "Would that it were I who could suffer the pain instead of you."

"I'm not complaining."

His head lowered to hers for a long, lingering kiss that fully aroused her husband. When his erection jutted against her, she lost all shyness, gathered her courage, and tenderly coiled her hand around his swollen shaft.

She hadn't realized how huge he could become, couldn't understand how that could fit inside of her.

He placed his hand over hers and initiated an up-and-down movement. With each thrust of her hand, her desire for him strengthened. A spurt of her own lubricated essence made her movements even more urgent.

Then he pushed away her hand as he slipped into her, his body fully joined with hers.

Later, once their normal breathing had been restored, her husband sighed and sat up, gazing down at her. "I'm most grateful I've wed the perfect wife. But we need to eat, and I've got to rush off to Parliament." He dropped a tender kiss on her forehead. "As much as I would enjoy spending the day in bed with you, I cannot."

"It's a pity we couldn't have had a wedding trip." Just the two of them, free to do whatever they liked, whenever they liked.

"I promise, when this session of Parliament is over, I'll take you wherever you want to go for a honeymoon."

Clutching the sheets to her chest, she also sat up, her back to him.

"I'll slip into my breeches and come back to assist you in dressing," he said.

Being naked in daylight was entirely different than being naked while making love bathed in firelight, different than lying beside him beneath the covers. Once her husband had returned to his bedchamber, she rushed to her dressing room and donned drawers and took the first steps toward putting on her stays. She would need his help lacing her up the back.

He came and stood in the doorway, smiling at her. "Allow me to help you." He laced her up, then dropped a nibbly kiss on her exposed neck. "I must not get started, you enticing creature. I have to attend today's session—and our breakfast is bound to be getting cold. Mustn't hurt Cook's feelings."

He was right. The breakfast offerings were tepid, but she cared not. She was too happy. She was confident in her husband's affection. Only one thing could have yielded total happiness: a declaration of his love. How she longed to hear those three words.

After slathering marmalade on his toast, he asked, "Have you given any more thought to what woman could be so mean-spirited toward you? Or who knew you were back in London?"

She was afraid he'd think her answer foolish, but this improbable scenario had persistently bothered her. "I know it sounds silly, but I keep thinking about the ghost."

"The ghost?"

"Yes, the beautiful woman who looked exactly like the Mrs. Powell I knew back in Devon—the one who died in the fire."

"You think it's possible she didn't die in that fire?"

She shrugged. "I suppose I am saying it's possible." She poured more tea for both of them.

"How would you explain that?"

"I don't know."

"Tell me again what you do know."

"Mrs. Powell was newly wed to the curate in the village of Manston Stoney. I've never seen a more beautiful woman. She came to our school twice a week to instruct the girls on the pianoforte. I expect she needed to supplement her husband's modest salary." She paused and sighed. "Then one night the little parsonage caught fire, and the two bodies were recovered the next day. It was most fortunate their maid had returned to her own village in Dorset just days before the fatal fire."

Her husband made no response for a moment, then he said, "What if it wasn't she who perished in the fire? What if the maid perished and not the beautiful Mrs. Powell?"

She gave him a quizzing look. "I don't understand."

"Perhaps she planned their deaths."

It was as if a bolt of lightning struck Georgiana. As horrifying as the suggestion was, it could explain why the woman on Piccadilly that day looked exactly like Mrs. Powell. It could also explain the way that woman had eyed Georgiana with unmistakable recognition before looking away and hurrying into her luxurious vehicle.

"Tell me again everything about that day on Piccadilly," he said.

She tried to picture the exact scene before she spoke. "At first, I was just admiring the woman's exquisite dress with matching pelisse and bonnet. Few women in London could afford anything that beautiful. Her bonnet had ostrich feathers dyed to match the lavender of her pelisse. At first I couldn't see her face, and when I did I was struck by how much she resembled Mrs. Powell. But I told myself it couldn't possibly be Mrs. Powell. I had attended her funeral."

"Though you wouldn't have actually seen the body because it would have been burned beyond recognition."

She nodded. "Then when I saw the unusual color of the woman's eyes, I had the eeriest feeling that Mrs. Powell had risen from the dead—which, of course, I knew was ridiculous. Still, I stumbled toward her."

"And that's when you plunged into the street." He smiled. "The luckiest day of my life."

"Mine, too," she whispered, stroking her husband's muscled forearm.

Their gazes locked. Warmth spread over her like a comforting blanket on a cold night.

"Please finish your tale," he said.

"As soon as our eyes met, she looked away and seemed to race to her waiting carriage. All I can tell you about the fine coach is that it bore a gold crest."

"You can't remember anything about the crest? Did it have an animal, like a stag or something?"

How she wished she had paid attention to it. She shook her head. "I couldn't say. The woman commanded all my attention."

He went to the sideboard, piled more food onto his plate, and returned to the table. "What if your Mrs. Powell is a calculated murderess?"

"The wife of a clergyman? I find that hard to believe."

"I'm thinking of the fine coach and the lovely clothes. Obviously, the woman you saw on Piccadilly was rich. What if your Mrs. Powell met another man? A rich man?"

"It's so . . . sinister."

"Yes, it is pure evil, but it would explain everything—especially the vendetta against you. If your Mrs. Powell is a murderess, she would fear exposure from you, hence the campaign to discredit you, to alienate you from Society." He set down his fork, a look of panic on his face. "And if she's killed two people already, she could . . ."

"She could want to kill me," Georgiana finished in a shaky whisper.

He nodded solemnly. "We've got to find that woman."

"First, ought we not try to prove that a murder occurred back in Manston Stoney?"

"You may get that wedding trip, after all. Tomorrow we go to Devon."

THAT AFTERNOON, LUCY and Harriett came to visit Georgiana. "We're gravely worried about these beastly things that are being printed about you in that disgusting *Gazette*," Lucy said. "Because I'm your sister and have always been with you, I know they're lies, but others don't know how exceedingly proper you are. You're being ruined. No one will receive you."

Georgiana had hoped that because of its reputation, not many would be reading the *Gazette*. This intelligence upset her greatly.

Her cousin Harriett nodded. "We came here directly after I asked that abominable Lady Gorington to leave my house. The woman pretended to be worried about the dreadful things the *Gazette* has been printing about my cousin."

Lucy nodded, her eyes narrowed to slits with anger. "The odious woman was gloating over your misfortune."

"Who can be responsible for those horrid things being printed about you?" Harriett asked.

Her stomach churning, Georgiana shrugged. "We don't

know. Who could even have known I was in London? I haven't seen anyone outside of family." She eyed Lucy. "Before I came, did you tell anyone I was coming to London?"

Lucy contemplated the question for a moment, then shook her head. "I'm quite sure I hadn't told anyone except for the upstairs maid who prepared your bedchamber."

Georgiana looked at her cousin. "What about you? Did you tell anyone?"

"No! I didn't even know you were coming."

"Charles wanted me to ask. We're most perplexed."

Before her sister and cousin left, Georgiana told them about the Mrs. Powell double and her plans to travel with her husband to Devon to investigate it.

CHAPTER THIRTEEN

T HIS WAS THE first time she and her husband had sat on the same seat in his carriage. She cuddled up to him beneath the rug early the next morning as they embarked on their journey to Devon, their coach rattling through the dark streets of London.

"How romantic it will be to share rooms at inns along the way," she said. She finally was getting a honeymoon! She would have Charles all to herself, every hour of every day. What heaven!

His arm settled around her. "Indeed it will. Will you be happy to be going back to Manston Stoney?"

"I spent almost no time in the village. The school I attended was very strict. One of the only times we were permitted to go to the village was to attend Mrs. Powell's funeral. I cried so much, my eyes were swollen for days. It was also the first time I'd been permitted to attend a funeral." She shrugged. "I have no good memories of Manston Stoney. I was very unhappy there. I had never been away from my family, and I missed them dreadfully."

He kissed her gloved hand. "It's a good thing females aren't allowed at burials. That would have done you in."

"Oh, dearest, I forgot to tell you that I did speak to my sister and cousin, Lady Harriett, and they assure me they didn't tell anyone I was coming to London."

He gave a solemn nod.

"I do hope we're wrong about Mrs. Powell," she said.

"Not as much as I do, but we need to know."

"What will we be looking for?"

He considered. "I think the key is the female servant. What do you know of her?"

"Nothing. I never met her. I just remember those at the funeral commenting about how fortunate it was she had returned to Dorset just before the awful tragedy."

"We will need to find out everything we can."

She was genuinely touched over her husband's concern for her. He had chosen her over his Parliamentary duties. One thing she had learned about Charles was his devotion to his duties. Duty always came first.

Was she even more important to him? He had been upset over the possibility of a threat to her life. It was wonderful to be sharing her life with this man who cared deeply for her.

She put her head upon his shoulder. They hadn't slept a lot last night. Once more, they had taken immense pleasure in their prolonged lovemaking.

Soon she went to sleep.

HE WASN'T SURE they would learn anything in Manston Stoney, but nothing had ever been more important to him than finding out the truth about Mrs. Powell. If there was any possibility his suspicions were right, the woman was capable of murdering the most precious person in his life. The very thought of such a danger sickened him. If anything happened to Georgiana, he would not want to live. It was impossible to love anyone more than he loved his wife. She had become necessary to his existence.

The contentment of having her close, of loving her and suspecting that she loved him, nearly overwhelmed him with powerful intensity. Each rise and fall of her breast as she dozed on his shoulder unfurled in him a heady sense of possession, of fulfillment few men would ever experience.

Several hours passed before she awakened, and he asked, "Are you hungry?"

"I am." She lifted the curtain and peered at the dreary, blustery landscape. "A pity it's so wretched a day. We won't be able to have a picnic."

He took the basket from the opposite seat and wedged it on the floor between their booted feet. "Cook saw to it that we would eat well."

Georgiana unwrapped a loaf of bread that was still warm all these hours later in spite of the day's chill. "I dare say she didn't get any sleep. This bread was freshly baked when we left at five this morning."

"She's a treasure."

Georgiana broke off a large chunk for him and a smaller one for herself.

"This time of year it gets dark so early, we'll have to stop for the night in just a couple of hours," he said.

She looked up at him and winked. "I hope you brought the chessboard to help us pass the time."

"I don't think we'll lack for something to do," he said with a grin.

THOSE THREE DAYS of their journey were the happiest of her life. During the coach rides, they learned much about each other. She found out that he was an only child born to an aging father and a much younger mother. They had hoped to give him siblings but failed. She learned that he and Freddie had been best friends since their first week at Eton when they were seven. She told him about growing up with her siblings and cousins, and they discussed authors and poets they both admired. He told her he did not enjoy high-stakes play—which was something of which she heartily approved. He told her of his aspirations to serve in government, and she vowed to be his helpmate in every way. Every word he'd said was stored in her memory, as precious as her late mother's pearls.

Their nights were spent in each other's arms with the bed curtains firmly closed around them and blankets piled on top to ward off the winter's chill.

They arrived in Manston Stoney at noon on the fourth day. Now it was time to find out about the mysterious Mrs. Powell.

CHAPTER FOURTEEN

S INCE THE GRAVEYARD was always by the village church, they
started there. Side-by-side tombstones marked the place
where the Reverend John Powell and Sarah Powell lay in eternal
rest. Georgiana stood there looking down at the stone markers as
a chill wind ripped through her. Her hooded, woolen cloak
offered little protection against the day's frosty cold. At least her
hands, sheathed with thick leather gloves and stuffed into an
ermine muff, were warm. Relatively.

She thought about digging up Mrs. Powell's casket. But what
good would that do after half a decade? She found herself
wondering if the corpse in that wooden box had the jet-black hair
of Mrs. Powell.

What color was the servant's hair? Georgiana wished she'd
had the opportunity to have met the girl.

She looked up at her husband. His great coat flapped in the
wind and his cheeks were rosy from the chill. His gaze had
moved to just beyond the tiny church. Though loose stones and
charred wood had been cleared away, the spot where the rectory
had stood bore a silent testimony to the tragedy that had
occurred there. "Is that where the rectory was?" he asked.

She would never forget the horror of seeing the burnt-down
cottage just behind the church that day she and her classmates
had attended the funeral. It looked vastly different these many

years later. The site had been cleared, and vegetation had sprung up where the cottage had once stood. But there was no mistaking its location. Of that, she was certain. "Yes."

Her gaze fanned over the property surrounding the village church. She remembered this scene perfectly from the day of the funeral.

"Shall we speak with some of the Powells' neighbors?" He proffered his arm.

She linked her arm through his, and they strode to a tiny, thatched cottage just west of the church. It was one of a handful of cottages surrounded by plots where gardens would grow in the spring. Maybe someone here would remember the Powells' servant from Dorset.

The presentation of Lord Churston's card brought a smile to the face of the aproned servant who answered the cottage door. The young woman was likely a few years older than Georgiana.

"My wife and I would like to claim a few minutes of your mistress's time," Charles said.

"I'm sure Mrs. Windworth will be delighted to speak with your lordship. Won't you come in?"

They took seats in the modest but spotless parlor while the mistress of the house was summoned. When a white-haired matron of advanced age shuffled into the chamber, Charles stood and introduced himself and Georgiana to the home's owner.

"I am Mrs. Windworth. Please, sit. To what do I owe the pleasure?" The elderly woman seated herself on the faded floral sofa.

Georgiana answered. "We were just passing through on our return from Cornwall, and I wanted to stop in the village where I'd gone to Miss Simpson's School for Exemplary Ladies. When I was a student here, I had the unpleasant experience of attending the Powells' funeral after that tragic fire."

Mrs. Windworth clutched at her breast and shook her head morosely. "It was such a horrible tragedy. Such a loss. There never was a lovelier creature than Mrs. Powell."

"I agree. For as long as I live, I shall never forget each feature of her incredible beauty," Georgiana said.

"Lady Churston was telling me that it was only by the greatest good fortune the life of their servant was spared," Charles said.

"Oh, yes! The girl—I remember her well. Her name was Annabelle Shaw. She had come to the Powells upon their marriage—when he was assigned to our little parish. I remember, too, that Annabelle came here as soon as she turned sixteen."

"I seem to recall hearing that she had returned to her family in Dorset?" Georgiana said.

"My own servant was shocked at being informed of that. You see, my servant—we call her Lulu—had become close friends with Annabelle, and Annabelle never told her she was returning to her family. I believe the girl's parents had fifteen children and could not afford to feed all those mouths."

"Do you recall what Miss Shaw looked like?" Charles asked.

"Poor thing was rather plain, but I suppose anyone would look plain next to the beautiful Mrs. Powell."

"I'm trying to remember her," Georgiana said. "What was her hair color?"

"It was a black as a raven."

Georgiana and Charles exchanged solemn gazes, their eyes widened.

"Was she small for her age?" Georgiana asked.

Mrs. Windworth thought a moment. "No. She was fully grown. Average size."

Georgiana continued with her inquiries. "Like the woman who employed her?"

"Yes, that's a good comparison. They were the same size. In fact, I remember once when Miss Shaw was gathering parsley in the garden, and I saw her from the back. I mistook her for Mrs. Powell."

"As we'll be traveling through Dorset," Georgiana said, "I thought we might stop and tell Miss Shaw about the Powells, let her know how fortunate she was to escape the tragedy. Do you remember where in Dorset she had lived?"

"I don't, but Lulu will." Mrs. Windworth reached for the bell and rang.

A moment later, the young woman in an apron returned.

"Lulu, can you tell these people where in Dorset Annabelle Shaw lived?"

"Yes, mum. She was from a village called Piddletown."

"Thank you," Charles said. "I understand you were friends with the girl."

"Yes, my lord."

"I suppose she told you why she was returning to her family?"

The young woman shook her head. "Not really, my lord."

"Oh," Charles said, half querying.

"'Twas actually the day after the fire I received a letter from Annabelle telling me 'er mum had summoned 'er 'ome."

"But you and she never discussed this in person?" Charles asked.

The servant named Lulu folded her mouth in a grim line. "No. I missed her dreadfully, but I was thankful she was spared."

"In these ensuing years, have you had any communication with her?" Charles asked.

Lulu did not answer for a moment. "I'm embarrassed to say, but I don't know 'ow to read and write. Mrs. Windworth 'ad to read the letter I received from Annabelle. I wanted to write 'er and let 'er know about the poor Powells, but I never did. I reckon Mrs. Powell, before she died, must 'ave written the letter to me for Annabelle. She didn't know how to write, neither."

Anger surged in Georgiana. Mrs. Powell must have written the letter to cover up her heinous crime.

"Would you have said the marriage between Mr. and Mrs. Powell was a happy one?" Charles asked, his gaze darting from Mrs. Windworth to her servant.

"I suppose it was. She was such a lovely woman. I'm sure Mr. Powell must have been devoted to her."

His gaze jumped to Lulu. "Was that your impression as well?"

The girl shrugged. "As far as I know the beautiful Mrs. Powell got along with 'er 'usband. He was, quite naturally, devoted to 'er. There was something sort of peculiar, though."

"What was that?" Charles asked.

"I once saw 'er gettin' in a fine coach belongin' to some wealthy lord. She didn't know I was watchin', and I sees her lookin' both ways before taking the gent's jeweled hand and climbing in."

"Is there a grand house hereabouts where a peer lives—or where a peer might visit?" Charles asked.

Both females shook their heads.

"How did you know the man was a lord?" Georgiana asked.

"'Cause there was one of them gold designs painted upon his shiny black carriage. It was one of those big carriages like a king would ride in. I've always been told that when you see one of them with the design on the door, you know it's for a lord or some royalty."

"Can you describe that gold design?" he asked.

She shook her head. "I was too far away, and I was mostly interested in Mrs. Powell."

"You said she took the lord's jeweled hand," Georgiana said. "Did you, perchance, notice a signet ring?"

"As I said, I was too far away."

Charles stood. "Come along, my love. We've taken enough of these kind people's time." Turning to them, he added, "Thank you very much for speaking with us today."

Outdoors, a chilled wind ripped through them, but Georgiana was oblivious to the discomfort. *Mrs. Powell is a murderess*, she kept thinking. Horrified.

Her husband walked beside her. "This is one time I am not happy to be proven right."

What he didn't say but what they both knew was that Georgiana's own life could be in jeopardy. She still didn't want to believe someone she had known could be guilty of so evil a plot.

"Does it not sound as if the beautiful Mrs. Powell had set her sights higher than a low-level clergyman?" he asked.

"It does. Oh, Charles, it's all so very awful!"

"I know." A moment later, he strove for levity. "I must commend my wife on her resourcefulness."

She gave him a mock glare. "You refer to my prevarications?"

"I had no idea you possessed such a talent for telling little white lies."

"I assure you, dearest, I'm normally a scrupulously honest person. But, you must own, a little lying is called for in today's situation."

"I agree. In fact, I hope to emulate you in the course of our inquiries. You might call it learning from a master."

She playfully swatted at him.

They walked toward the cemetery again. Not ten yards in, she stumbled on an ancient, unreadable headstone, and fell to the ground. Fortunately, she landed on soil instead of stone, but on the way down, she'd tried to block the fall by reaching for the headstone, which leaned even further askew from her weight. Her left glove tore, and little drops of blood beaded her scraped palm.

Her husband, concern etched on his face, dropped down next to her. "Are you hurt?"

She let out a big sigh. "I warned you. I'm hopelessly clumsy, but I am blessed with good bones."

"How do you know you've not broken something since you haven't tried to stand? Come," he said, getting to his feet. "Allow me to help you up."

She groaned as she got to her feet, and then recovering, she twirled around to demonstrate she had suffered no ill effects from her spill. "All I sustained was a muddied dress and embarrassment. What a sight I'll make at tonight's inn."

"Peg will fix you up." Peg and Thorne had come along in another coach to see to their employers' needs and to provide fresh bed linens along the way.

"I wonder who Mrs. Powell's lord is," she said.

"That is, indeed, our quest. If Lulu saw that clandestine meeting between Mrs. Powell and the lord, perhaps someone else here in Manston Stoney also did."

"Brilliant! We must talk to more residents."

This time they went to a house on the other side of the church. It was another thatched, wattle and daub house. Charles knocked upon the well-worn door that had once been white but was now peeling and yellowed. Dogs barked and children squealed as the mistress of the house came to open the door.

Charles presented his card. "Could Lady Churston and I ask you a few questions?"

The woman, who looked to be in her mid-twenties, patted at her unkempt, sand-colored coif. "Please, my lord, Won't you come into my parlor? I beg that you forgive the untidiness. It's difficult to keep a house tidy when one has four young ones." She spoke with a genteel accent, as had Mrs. Windworth.

Once more, Georgiana told her about attending school in Manston Stoney and attending the Powells' funeral. "As we were passing through, I wanted to stop and pay my respects at their graves. Did you know the deceased?"

"We knew Mr. Powell from the Sunday services. They died just before Mr. Harding and I married."

"What of Mrs. Powell?" Georgiana asked.

"I never really spoke to her but, of course, knew who she was. I never saw anyone so lovely. Such a sad shame that beautiful creature died in the fire."

"Let me ask you," Charles said, "I was told that back around the time of the tragic fire, a noble friend of mine may have spent some time here, but I can't for the life of me remember which friend it was. Did you ever see his fine, crested coach in Manston Stoney? This would have been five or six years ago."

"We so rarely have crested coaches visit Manston Stoney, having no stately homes hereabouts, so seeing one definitely commands attention. But I do remember one from a half a dozen years ago. I thought the titled man must be a friend of Mrs. Powell's because more than once, I saw her climb into his impressive coach."

Just as Georgiana thought!

"What a great memory you possess," Charles said. "Now if you could take it a step further. Do you remember what the crest looked like?"

"If you'd have asked me five or six years ago, I may have remembered, but too much time has passed. I remember nothing about it." A toddler, lugging a woolen blanket behind him, came to his mother and climbed upon her lap. She unconsciously pressed a kiss on top his blond head as he contentedly shoved a thumb into his mouth.

It was such a simple scene, but it melted something inside of Georgiana. How she would love to have her own little son, a little Charles. The very contemplation of it left her heart fluttering, her spirits buoyed. She'd never known such happiness as she had during the past few days.

"Did you know the peer's name?" Georgiana asked.

The young mother shook her head. "I never knew it."

"Mama!" a little girl of about four shrieked as she ran into the parlor. "Harry drank the last of the milk, and you told him not to!"

"Run along, Phoebe. I'll deal with your brother after these fine people leave."

The little girl's gaze flicked to Charles, then to Georgiana before she hung her head and left the chamber.

"Well," Charles said, standing, "it's very kind of you to speak with us. Thank you very much."

When they were far enough away from the house not to be heard, Georgiana said, "It does sound like Mrs. Powell was having an affair."

"If we're right, she concocted a deadly plot to extricate herself from the marriage in order to wed the obviously wealthy peer."

"I truly hope we're wrong."

"We must find out for sure."

The sun was sinking. "We'll go back to that inn we passed outside of Exeter. Then tomorrow we go to Dorset."

To the village of Piddletown to see if Annabelle ever did return home.

CHAPTER FIFTEEN

DAWN WAS BREAKING when they left the inn the next morning. "I'm encouraged that we may be able to make Piddletown late this afternoon," Charles told his wife.

"I know we must go, know we must prove our suspicions, but I believe we both know what we're going to learn there," she said, placing her hand possessively on his thigh.

He nodded. "If we are proved correct, we'll have to tell the Shaws we believe their daughter's dead. That's not going to be easy."

"I don't think I'll be able to do it."

"I will."

The slight movement of her hand on his thigh was having a noticeable effect on him.

"I can always count on you," she said, tracing sultry circles on the muscles between his knee and groin.

It pleased him that she understood he would always put her and her needs first and that they had come to really know each other during this journey. He'd been prepared to marry her solely because of her beauty, though his decision to marry her could have been aided by her being a member of the illustrious Beresford family—not for the money but because his parents would be so pleased. Now he knew that without a doubt he had the perfect wife.

Had Charles set out to find the ideal woman to be his life's companion, to bear his children, he could not have found anyone better than Georgiana. Nor could he ever have loved another woman as he loved her.

He put his arm around her. "Would you object if I wanted to kiss you?" he asked in a low, husky voice.

She answered with actions instead of words. Her gaze searing, she moved her face close to his and flattened her hand against his chest.

Her touch had the most profound effect upon him. His lips lowered to hers for a soft kiss. Her lips eagerly parted beneath his, and her breath began to grow ragged. He would never have believed the passion that lay beneath his fair Georgiana's graceful countenance. In the last several nights he had finally come to understand the power Delilah had over Samson, for his wife had just such a power over him.

His lovely Georgiana had enslaved him, and he wasn't sure he liked being so subservient to his passion, so drugged by her lovemaking that at times he thought he could forget everything except the pleasure of her luscious body.

This was one of those times. Despite it being daytime, and despite the fact that his coachman, though unseen, was less than six feet away, Charles wanted her. He wanted her so badly it overpowered every ounce of his self-control.

What governed this passion was the knowledge that she wanted him as badly as he wanted her. Without breaking the kiss, his hands spanned her waist, and he hoisted her onto his lap, and his hand slid beneath her skirts, edging up the smooth flesh of her thighs.

She made a little moaning noise as her thighs parted further. She flung off the cloak which had suddenly become too hot. She looked at him with those smoldering eyes.

"Allow me to help unfasten your dress." He carefully unfastened the back of her dress, then lowered it and her stays until her breasts sprang free, and he bent to suckle on a pink nipple.

He could explode with want. He spoke with a gently commanding voice. "Saddle me as you would a horse."

Her gaze dreamy, she placed a leg on either side of him as his hands moved greedily beneath her skirts. When he found her warm and wet, he knew he could not wait another minute.

As he started to free himself from his breeches, she reached to help. Feeling her hand glide along his rigid length sent him over his controlled edge.

Seconds later, he entered her in one smooth surge as her arms gripped him and she began to thrash against his torso.

She had taken him to heaven's gate many times, but this time he was sure they were going beyond the brink. This time the power of their mating equaled the surge of an earthquake or a tidal wave or an immensely powerful storm that man could not control.

He gloried in the feel of her shuddering over him, in the moisture that dampened her sable hair, and the rivulets that streamed down her face and between her breasts.

He held her tight as she convulsed against him, and when her breath returned to normal, he allowed himself the luxury of tasting her other nipple.

As his own breath steadied, he vowed not to take her again. Not here in the carriage. Already he wondered if the coachman had heard her moans. Had he felt their frenzied rocking? What could Charles have been thinking to throw propriety to the wind? His wife deserved to have her ladylike image better guarded. Especially after the wicked things that had been written about her in the *Gazette*.

The last thing Charles wanted was for his coachmen to start fantasizing about Lady Churston. Charles chided himself for not being more protective of her reputation.

She sank against him. Even though it was a cold winter day, he could have wrung out her dress, it was so drenched. Had she stood in a rainstorm, her hair could not have been wetter. He smoothed away the soggy hair from her brow and planted soft kisses on her warm forehead.

There was so much he wanted to tell her. He wanted to tell her how much he loved her. He wanted to tell her he worshiped the very ground she trod. He wanted to tell her he could never have loved anyone else with the intensity with which he loved her. But, as much as he wanted to tell her these things, he could not.

Even though he was certain she cared for him, he was terrified he would lose her affections if she perceived him a weakling. Might she think him less manly if he allowed her to know of his nearly debilitating need? His all-encompassing devotion?

He couldn't afford the risk.

He tucked himself back into his breeches and then began to help restore her clothing. Her skin was damp and cold now. When he finished, he lovingly wrapped her in the woolen shawl.

⟫⟫⟫✺⟪⟪⟪

LATE THAT AFTERNOON they crossed the River Piddle. "Did you know that piddle is a Saxon word?" Georgiana asked.

Just one more thing he loved about her. She was well read and intelligent. "I did not. What's it mean?"

"Clear water."

"And you know that because . . . ?"

She shrugged. "It must be a piece of useless knowledge I picked up at that school in Devon."

Moments later they reached the tiny village of Piddletown. Not a single commercial building could be found on the high street. He suspected those attached, thatched houses that lined the street had been in the same family for generations.

The coachman had been instructed to ask where the Shaws' house could be found. On the high street, the coach stopped, and the driver called out to a woman wearing a red woolen cloak, its hood covering her graying head as she closed her house's door behind her. "Where might I find the Shaw's residence?" he asked.

"Which Shaw would that be?"

That was when Charles remembered that Annabelle Shaw had a large number of siblings. Some of her brothers were bound to be grown now and living in their own houses. He opened his coach window and spoke to the woman himself. "We were looking for the Shaw family that included, I believe, fifteen children."

She nodded, her gaze lingering on his coach's crest. "That would be Martha Shaw. She lost 'er 'usband last year. She lives right here on the high street, though most of 'er young ones have gone off to lives of their own now." She pointed across the street. "Hers is the one with the blue door."

"Thank you," Charles said. He turned to Georgiana and blew out a breath. "This is it. Would you care to wager on the outcome?"

"No. I feel certain I know what we're going to find out, and I have no wish to glory in this family's misfortune."

A moment later, he was tapping at the blue door. A plump woman of about fifty answered. As had become his custom, he handed her his card. Her gaze went from it to his fine carriage parked across the street.

"Lady Churston and I would like a word with the Mrs. Shaw who's the mother of Annabelle Shaw." His gut tightened.

"That would be me." She held open the door. "Won't you come in to my 'umble abode?"

He had expected Annabelle Shaw's parents to be older. This woman looked to be in her middle fifties. He supposed Annabelle would now be around two-and-twenty or three-and-twenty.

She showed them into her parlor. Its wooden floors, like the half a dozen pieces of furniture here, were worn smooth in places from years of use. The curtains had faded so much that it was now impossible to tell what they must have once looked like. He and Georgiana chose to sit upon simple wood side chairs close to the door.

"I do hope you 'aven't brought me bad news about me girl."

He couldn't bring himself to answer for a moment, and when he did, he hadn't the heart to share his suspicions with her. "I never met your girl, but we were told in Manston Stoney that she was from Piddletown, and as we were passing by so close, we thought we'd stop by and pay a visit."

"If you never met me girl, why did you want to pay 'er family a visit?"

"It may sound silly, but I was intrigued over the name of the village she came from, and since we were close . . . well, here we are. How long since you saw Annabelle?"

"We 'aven't laid eyes on her since her sixteenth birthday, the day she left."

His gut plummeted. Even though he knew the answer, he felt compelled to keep this conversation going. "And how long ago was that?"

"When one has fifteen young ones, it's sometimes hard to keep up with all them birthdays. I reckon it was at least five years ago. No, wait! She was born exactly two years before our baby, Jeremiah." Her eyes sparkled. "He just turned one-and-twenty, and he now has a young one of his own and his own house, too, over near the river. I wish all my children had been able to stay in Piddletown like him. So I'm guessing my sweet Annabelle left 'ere about seven years ago. I 'ope she's doing well."

What a coward he was! He couldn't tell the woman her daughter had been murdered. Wouldn't it be best to allow her think Annabelle was doing well? "She's very well thought of in Manston Stoney." That much was true. He'd not heard a bad word about her.

"I bet my Annabelle wanted you to stop by and see how 'er family is getting along. You can let 'er know her Papa passed last winter. It's been . . . well, I can't take another loss. It would kill me, I'm sure."

Thank God he hadn't told her the truth. "I'm sorry for your loss, but it must be a comfort to have some of your children near."

"It is. And I've got four-and-twenty grandchildren in and around Piddletown."

"We just heard from your neighbor there were many Shaws living here," Georgiana said, standing. "You are blessed to have a large family."

He stood, and Georgiana linked her arm to his. "Lord Churston and I have only recently married, but I would feel so fortunate if he and I could be blessed with fifteen children, like you, Mrs. Shaw."

The older woman smiled upon them. "Children are greater than diamonds and pearls. I hope you do get that large family."

They had not directly discussed having children, but Georgiana's comment did not surprise him. Until she'd spoken of it, he hadn't realized how much he would welcome a child of theirs. The contemplation of it was rather better than his horse winning the Derby.

When they returned to their coach, Georgiana's sympathetic gaze met his. "I'm glad you didn't tell her. Let her think Annabelle is happy in Devon."

"I've learned something else just now."

"What?"

"I'm not leaving you alone until we sort out all this wickedness. That evil Mrs. Powell is capable of killing—" he paused, swallowed, then continued, "—the most important person in my life."

CHAPTER SIXTEEN

T HE SUN WAS not shining during this last leg of their journey. Even the rug spread across their laps could not ward off the chill that seeped into her very bones. Nevertheless, Georgiana felt as if this were the most glorious day of her life. Charles had unfurled his stiffness and made passionate love to her here in the coach. And then, later, he had told her she was the most important thing in his life!

Each day of this journey had brought her increasingly more happiness. "It has been a true wedding trip, my darling," she said.

He squeezed her hand. She had hoped he would concur or make a declaration, but he said nothing. For now she would be satisfied with his determination to protect her.

"I know you're concerned for my safety, but you can't be with me every minute when we return to London," she said. "There are your parliamentary duties to consider."

"I meant it when I told you there's nothing more important right now than preserving the life of my wife."

Since the day they had wed, she had longed to hear him tell her he loved her. She was still waiting for those words, but she thought what he'd just told her was even more romantic. A man who felt that way about his wife had to be a man who was in love with his wife.

She felt as if she could soar to the heavens. This man she had married most definitely caused the *champagne effect*. In spades.

"What do you propose to do next—regarding Mrs. Powell?" she asked.

"We've got to find out who she is now."

"It's almost a certainty she's married a titled man."

"Yes. One wonders if that man of supposedly high rank may have been involved with the murders in Manston Stoney."

"It is a very real possibility. I think it's been proven that she knew him before she supposedly perished."

"Let us speculate on a possible scenario."

She nodded. "Exceptionally beautiful young wife who's living on a meager income catches the eye of a nobleman passing through."

"She's flattered by his attentions."

"And by his wealth."

"He becomes obsessed with possessing her."

"But, being a man of high standing, he cannot marry a divorced woman." Georgiana looked thoughtful. "Divorced women are not accepted in Society, and this aristocrat wishes to flaunt his new wife's beauty like a chest full of medals."

"Good."

"So . . . together they concoct the plan that this woman of insignificant birth dies in the fire—along with her clergyman husband."

"But, of course, she doesn't die," he continued. "Their maid, who was the same size and possessed of the same hair color as Mrs. Powell, is substituted for her. And just before the tragedy, Mrs. Powell writes a note to Annabelle Shaw's friend, Lulu, saying she has returned to Piddletown."

"And everyone believes that poor Mr. and Mrs. Powell had the misfortune to die in the tragic fire."

"While meanwhile the peer marries the beautiful woman and returns to London to proudly display his lovely bride."

"It all sounds so plausible," she said. "And so very tragic. Do you think Mrs. Powell is now a countess or a marchioness?"

"It certainly seems possible. I suppose she could even be a duchess."

"Do you know, that day I saw her on Piccadilly, I had the feeling I was observing a duchess. There was such superiority in her bearing, such unmistakable wealth in her clothing, such a high quality in her spotless carriage."

"Then when we get home, we'll go through *Debrett's* and enumerate the highest-ranking men who are known to reside at least part of the year in London. We'll pay particularly close attention to the information about the spouses, especially ones with her name. I know we saw it on the gravestone, but I didn't really pay attention. Did you?

"Her Christian name is Sarah. Starting with *Debrett's* is a great idea."

THEY DIDN'T ARRIVE at their London home until night, and both were exhausted. Before he went to bed, Charles gathered the servants together and stressed that all doors and windows must be locked at all times. "And," he added, "no one is permitted in the house without the permission of Lady Churston or myself. The only exceptions are my wife's cousins, Lord and Lady Devere and Lord and Lady Rockingham, along with her sister, Lady Montague, or her spouse. Also, my friend Freddie Fortescue. Though my wife's brother and younger sister have returned to the country, anyone named Beresford is to be admitted."

Now that he knew what kind of evil the former Sarah Powell was capable of, he worried more than ever about Georgiana's safety.

When he went upstairs, the noxious odor told him that in their absence the painters had begun painting the viscountess's bedchamber. He opened Georgiana's chamber door to discover the room in disarray with heavy canvases thrown across all the furnishings.

In his bedchamber, Georgiana had slipped into his bed. "I'll be here until my bedchamber's finished. Is the smell not wretched?"

He chuckled. "When I was a lad, I loved the smell of fresh paint."

"And now?"

"Not so much." He tossed off his jacket, then untied his cravat. "If you don't want Thorne in here, my dear, you may have to assist me in removing these boots. I have a devil of time doing it myself."

She left the bed and stooped in front of him as he plopped on the chair.

His breath hitched as he watched her leave the bed, the silhouette of her perfect body visible beneath the thin night rail. When she bent to help remove one boot, her full breasts fell from the low-cut nightclothes.

With thoughts of making love to his wife, his tiredness vanished like the flame of a snuffed candle. Which is what he did once his boots were removed.

MIDWAY THROUGH BREAKFAST, Freddie called. Charles stuffed a quarter of a muffin into his mouth, grabbed his cup of tea, stood, and brushed his lips across Georgiana's cheek. "I'll be in the library with Freddie, if you need me."

In the library, a miffed Freddie greeted him. "You were gone a whole, bloody week!"

"I know very well how long I was gone. Sit down so I can fill you in on what we have discovered."

The two men sat close to the fire, Charles on the sofa and his friend in a chair near the hearth. "Feels good," Freddie said, shaking his head. "Beastly cold out there today."

"It's definitely one of those days one doesn't want to get out of bed."

"You missed quite a bit of parliamentary action while you were gone."

Charles eyed the newspapers that had piled up on his desk. "I'll read the accounts in the newspapers in an attempt to catch up, but I won't be attending sessions for a while."

"Why not?"

"Because my wife's life may be in danger, and I'll not leave her." Charles proceeded to tell his friend details about the chilling crime they'd pieced together during their journey.

Freddie's eyes widened. "Murdering a clergyman and an innocent girl of sixteen! Diabolical."

"It is, indeed. I'll be asking for your help as we try to discover the new identity of the wicked murderess."

"You going to kill her when you find the she-devil?"

"Of course not! Though she certainly deserves it. I'll let the proper authorities handle her."

"Is that wise? Her husband's apparently a man of influence."

"So are the Beresfords—and, I'd like to think, the Churstons."

"Right you are."

"I don't need to tell you that everything I've shared with you this morning is to be shared with no one. My wife's life is at stake. We can't take a chance on this getting back to the one I'm seeking."

"The she-devil. Do you not think her lordly husband—the new one, not to be confused with the deceased one, who has likely already met his heavenly Lord—might have had a hand in the murders?"

"It's a very real possibility."

"What can I do to help?"

"First off, be on the lookout for what everyone describes as an extremely beautiful woman of high rank."

Freddie's face brightened. "Now that's an assignment I shall embrace. *Extremely beautiful* you say?"

"That's how everyone describes her. She is said to be possessed of black hair, pale blue eyes, and an exquisite body, and is not past the age of thirty. She also dresses very well, but I'm not sure you know anything about ladies' fashions."

"Are you saying that because I have no history with ladies other than opera dancers?"

Charles shrugged. "Feel free to correct me if I've erred. Do you know what kind of clothes the women of our class consider fashionable?"

Freddie stuck out his lower lip. "Bloody expensive ones."

"Not good enough an answer."

"I suppose there are those who would consider me clueless about fashions worn by well-born women."

"That's because you don't associate with well-born women."

Freddie screwed up his face. "You going to make me go to Almack's?"

"I know how much you dislike that. I'm also guessing that our she-devil may be avoiding that place because she has no desire to be seen by my wife. She would know the Beresfords are a powerful family and would be expected to attend the assemblies at Almack's."

Relief rushed over Freddie. "So I'm just to be keeping my eyes and ears open in order to locate the evil beauty?"

"Right. As our investigation progresses, I'm sure I may be calling on you to aid me in other ways."

Freddie stood. "You can count on me."

As SOON AS Freddie left, Georgiana came swishing into the library. "Where's the *Debrett's*?"

He went to the library shelf where he kept the thick book.

"How old is your edition?" she asked. "We need one that's been recently published."

He looked at the flyleaf. "It was published two years ago."

"That should do. The former Mrs. Powell must have married her lord around five years ago. Possibly six."

"When was the fire at the parsonage?"

"Now, let me see. I was only at the Devon school for one year. I went there about six months after I turned thirteen, and I left about six months after I turned fourteen. I'm sure the fire must have been six years ago."

He eyed her affectionately. "It must have been shortly after you left Devon that I met you."

She gave him a quizzing look that bordered on hostile. "You met me before?"

"Well, we didn't actually meet, but I took notice of James's sister, who he reminded me was only fourteen."

Her mouth dropped open. "The cricket match at Eton!"

"Yes."

"You really did take notice of me that day?"

"I did. I thought you were without question the prettiest of all the sisters in attendance."

"My dear Lord Churston, you will put me to the blush!"

"I shall be offended that you didn't notice me that day," he teased.

"I was rather lad mad and excited to be around so many fine-looking young fellows that day. I loved every minute of it, but I confess I don't remember you."

"I'm grateful that has now been rectified." He dropped a soft kiss on her rosy lips.

She opened a drawer in his writing table. "I believe I'll get a large sheet of parchment and start a list of possibilities. It's a bit of a pity her first name is Sarah. It seems as if every other peer is married to a Sarah."

"I'm hoping that's an exaggeration."

"It is, but it's not far from the mark."

He took the book to the large writing table that backed up to the sofa. "We can work here." Two chairs were already tucked beneath it.

He thumbed through the pages and groaned. "There are hundreds of entries."

"I know, but at least we can eliminate all who are not married to a Sarah."

He sighed. "It has just occurred to me that in an attempt to completely hide her former identify, she may have adopted a new Christian name."

Georgiana shut her eyes as if she were in pain. "In that case, I shall borrow your razor from Thorne and slash my wrists."

"This is no joking matter."

"I know. What you've suggested is a very real possibility."

They sat down, side by side. "At this point we need to concentrate on peers married to Sarah."

"I agree."

It would be a monumental task. He had not exaggerated when he said there were hundreds—if not thousands—of entries. "It's a good thing we've got all day."

"Or all week," she said in all earnestness.

"It would have helped if someone in Manston Stoney had seen the peer and could have given us some idea of his age."

"It most certainly would have, and . . ." she pretended to glare at him, "it would have helped had you been more social. If you and Freddie spent less time in gentlemanly pursuits like race meetings, cock fights, and nights at Brook's and more time at balls and assemblies with the *ton,* you would know several of these peers' wives."

"You've got me there."

"I've thought of one thing we can eliminate." Her eyes flashed with excitement.

"What?"

"Every peer's wife who hails from an aristocratic family can be dismissed. We know Mrs. Powell was not of our class."

"What if she lied?"

Georgiana shook her head. "I don't think she could get away with that. It's too easy to disprove."

"I expect you're right." He nodded thoughtfully. "I believe I'll eliminate viscounts and baronets also. At least for now."

"I have rather a fondness for viscounts," she said playfully.

"But many of us won't be very wealthy until our fathers die. It was your impression the woman you believe is Sarah Powell is extremely wealthy."

"True." She gave a shrug of resignation. "Go ahead and dismiss viscounts."

"So we'll look at dukes, marquesses, and earls. What about barons?"

She thought a moment. "I know the late Lord Holland's father was extremely wealthy, and the Hollands are barons."

"So we know barons can be quite wealthy. We'll keep them in our search. Are we ready to begin?" he asked.

"Yes. Do you propose going alphabetically?"

"Might as well."

"I've thought of one more thing that will help us narrow our search."

He gave her a quizzing look. "What?"

"They always list the date of the peer's marriage. We can eliminate any couples married more than six years ago."

"Good suggestion."

She scooted closer to him so she could see the entries at the same time he did. On the first few pages, she rolled her eyes. "Is it really necessary to trace each family tree back practically to the Saxons?"

"My wife exaggerates."

She sighed. "At least Lord Abernathy's wife is not named Sarah. Let's move along at a faster rate."

Over the next few minutes, they became adept at quickly checking for the name and lineage of each peer's wife as indicated by the lower-case m., indicating "married," that preceded the peer's wife's name.

"Well, it looks like Lord Amherst is the first one who's married to a Sarah." She looked up at her husband. "Have you met them?"

"If you looked more carefully, you'd see he resides in Canada."

"Oh."

He thumbed through several more pages.

"I take back what I said about half the peers being married to women named Sarah," she said. "I see now that Elizabeths outnumber Sarahs significantly," she said.

"I'm thankful Mrs. Powell wasn't named Elizabeth."

"I'm even seeing more Margarets than Sarahs."

A moment later, she said, "Oh, look! Lord Bryson is married to a Sarah. Do you know either of them?"

He looked at the family information, puckering his lips. "He's an earl. Can't say that I know him. I wish my father were here. He'd know any man who served in the House of Lords. Oh, forget it. His Sarah is the daughter of the Marquess of Stoneham."

"That certainly lets out our Sarah. Though I hate to call her *our* Sarah, given that she's so wicked."

For the next hour, every Sarah they found was the daughter of a man of high rank. Every. Single. One.

The first one who fit within the perimeters of their search was the wife of the Duke of Dorchester. According to the entry, this duke's wife was the daughter of Col. Thomas Brandywine of India.

"This is very promising," she said. "No one can check the veracity of this claim. Is that not something our Mrs. Powell would do?"

"Indeed it is."

"Do you know the Duke of Dorchester?"

He shook his head as he continued to read the lengthy entry. "The man is older. With this birth date, he'd be about ten years older than me."

"Very promising, indeed." Georgiana wrote down the duke's name. "We'll ask Devere about him."

"I'd almost forgotten my family now includes such a prominent member of the House of Lords," he said.

For the next two hours, they continued. His neck ached from perpetually looking down. He was getting hungry. They'd been at this for nearly four hours and only had one name on their list.

"We need to take a break," he said.

"Let's go sit by the fire for a few minutes. Would you like something sweet to eat?"

"A capital idea! Did Cook not have fresh plum pudding waiting for us last night when we arrived home?"

"Indeed she did. I'll ring."

He sat on the sofa near the fire. Glad he was not to have to leave his house on so cold a day. After Georgiana told the footman to fetch her husband's sweet, she came to stand behind Charles, kneading his neck.

What had he ever done to deserve this woman? No man could have a finer wife. "Thank you. That feels wonderful. Your hands are magic."

The footman soon arrived with his plate of plum pudding, and she came to sit next to Charles while he ate. "Would you care for a bite?" he asked.

"One."

After he cleaned his plate, he said, "We need to get back to our search." He could think of several other things he'd rather be doing, but it was as if their lives were at a standstill until he could make sure his wife was out of danger.

They worked until the footman came into the chamber to light the candles as night was falling. During the afternoon, they had found three more possibilities.

The first was another duke. The Duke of Harkey, a man in his fifties, was married to a Sarah, the daughter of a Barbados plantation owner who was not identified.

The next was the Earl of Rhonson, who married Sarah, the daughter of the Rev. Hollister. No location given for the reverend.

The last was the Marquess of Williers, whose Sarah was the

daughter of another colonel, this one residing in Canada.

Charles frowned. "I must own, all four sound suspicious."

"Let's go to Devere House. My cousin is bound to know at least some of those men."

CHAPTER SEVENTEEN

I N DEVERE'S LIBRARY, Georgiana and Charles explained to her cousin their suspicions about the former Mrs. Powell's unconscionable crimes and their efforts to prove them. "Because Georgiana can identify her, we believe she's responsible for the written attacks against Georgiana in the *Gazette*," Charles said.

"This is without a doubt the most fiendish plot I've ever had personal knowledge of," Devere said, "but you make a most compelling case against the woman. It was clever of you to go to Devon and Dorset to try to get at the root of the evil scheme, but how do you propose to find out her identity?"

They told him about their search of *Debrett's*.

"Have we convinced you?" Georgiana asked.

"Indeed you have. I'm bursting with curiosity to find out which aristocratic families you've whittled down your search to."

Lady Devere, who sat beside her husband on the sofa, had a question. "Let's assume you are convinced beyond any doubt of the true Sarah Powell, how can you possibly prove it?"

Georgiana answered. "I, for one, could identify her—as can several who live in Manston Stoney."

"She will deny it," Caroline, Lady Devere said.

"Another idea has come to me," Devere said.

Charles eyed his wife's cousin. "Go on."

"As she's already committed two murders, she may try to kill

Georgiana, too. If she should make such an attempt, you could then catch her in the act of trying to commit a third murder. That would be irrefutable proof of her guilt."

Charles's hands coiled into fists. His eyes narrowed to slits. Anger surged through him. "You suggest I simply sit by and allow my wife to be thrust into further danger?"

"I know there's a certain amount of risk involved with this sort of plan, but you, me, Monty, Rockingham, your friend Freddie Fortescue—all of us can assist in guarding Georgiana. James, too. I'm sure he'd rush to London to help protect his sister. We can ensure that she'd be guarded around the clock."

"I won't consider such a plan," Charles said angrily.

"If the woman is as evil and unscrupulous as you believe," Caroline said, "she may already be plotting a way to permanently silence Georgiana."

"That's why I'll not leave my wife's side until that woman is in prison," Charles said.

"Do you think the woman's husband could have been in on the scheme?" Devere asked.

"We don't know," Georgiana answered.

"Though it's very likely," Charles added.

"If he's wealthy enough and powerful enough to ensure a newspaper does his bidding," Devere said, "what's to prevent him from employing a bunch of cut-throats to eliminate Georgiana?"

Charles's gaze flicked to his wife. Her face blanched, her lips quivered, and she clutched at his hand, holding it so hard, her knuckles whitened. It tore into his heart to see her like this, but even more terrifying was the prospect that he could lose her to a mad woman's evil scheme. "I would lay down my life to protect her."

"We all feel that way," Devere said in a gentle voice, tossing a solemn look at his frightened cousin. "Let's see if I'm familiar with any of the names you've come up with."

Georgiana unfurled her sheet of parchment. "We have two dukes. The first is the Duke of Dorchester, who married his Sarah six years ago. It said she was the daughter of a colonel serving in India." She looked up at her cousin. "Do you know the Duke of Dorchester?"

"I do," Devere said. "He sometimes attends sessions in the House of Lords. He's a Tory. I don't believe I've ever seen him in a social setting. Have no idea what his wife looks like."

"*Debrett's* gave his age as five-and-thirty," Charles said.

"Yes, he's a little older than I am. If he attended Eton, it would have been before I arrived."

Almost all the men of their acquaintance had attended Eton, though Charles did know many peers' sons went to Harrow and Westminster. "Would you say he's wealthy?"

"Oh, yes. Very."

"We need to find out where he lives," Charles suggested.

Devere directed his attention to his cousin. "Who's the other duke?"

"The Duke of Harkey. Do you know him?"

"I've never met him, but he's said to be enormously wealthy."

"*Debrett's* said he was fifty," Georgiana said.

"What did you learn about his wife?" Devere asked.

"She was the daughter of an unnamed plantation owner in Barbados."

"Another suspicious entry," Devere said.

"Do you know if the duke spends time in London?" Charles asked.

Devere shook his head morosely. "I feel so useless. I've never met the fellow, wouldn't know him if he walked right up to me. But I seem to have heard that he does spend time in London."

"The man is closer to your father's age," Georgiana said. "You can't be expected to know him. Besides, it's said there are ten thousand members of Britain's aristocratic families. Of course, you can't know them all."

"And since the majority of peers are Tories, chances are the titled man we seek will be a Tory," Charles said. "So he'd be more inclined to go to White's, and I spend most of my time at Brook's."

"There is that."

"Let's finish that list before we begin speculating," Charles said.

Georgiana consulted her list again. "The Earl of Rhonson. His wife is said to be the daughter of the Reverend Hollister, no location given. The wedding occurred five years ago."

Devere nodded. "That sounds promising."

"But, dearest," Lady Devere said, "I've met Lady Rhonson, and I don't think anyone would describe her as beautiful. You did say the evil Sarah Powell was extraordinarily beautiful, did you not?" she asked Georgiana.

"Extraordinarily beautiful describes her perfectly."

"If she's that beautiful," Devere said playfully, "I would remember her. Please describe her."

"Average height, perfect figure, black hair, and her blue eyes are an unusual and striking shade of blue like my sister Lucy's."

"Then they are beautiful," Caroline said, "for they're definitely Lucy's best feature."

"And the day I saw the woman I believed to be Sarah Powell on Piccadilly, she was dressed exquisitely," Georgiana added.

Devere screwed up his face in thought. "I believe I'd remember if I'd seen a woman possessed of such beauty." He looked lovingly at his bride. "As you can see, I'm noted for my taste for in beautiful women."

Lady Devere smiled at her husband.

"And who do we having rounding out that list?" Devere asked his cousin.

"That would be the Marquess of Williers." She looked at her cousin for confirmation.

He made no sign that the name was familiar to him.

She read on. "According to *Debrett's*, his wife Sarah, whom he married three years ago, is the daughter of a British colonel who now resides in Canada. No name given."

"That sounds awfully suspicious," Devere said, "and the

marriage did occur within the years you're looking at." He shook his head. "I can tell you the marquess has never taken his seat in the House of Lords."

"I wonder how we find out if he has a London residence," Georgiana said.

"I'll start by asking about him at Brook's." Devere eyed Charles. "I know you can't go because you won't leave your wife, and I commend your decision to guard over her."

"It's disappointing that you don't know these," Charles said. "We counted on you knowing everyone who's anyone in the Capital."

Devere chuckled. "You imbue me with qualities I do not possess." He paused to consider. "There are just a handful of locations in London where aristocrats live. There are the squares, like your Berkeley Square, Churston, and Grosvenor Square, Cavendish Square, and Manchester Square. I think I know everyone on Curzon, and Rockingham knows everyone on Half Moon. I believe all of us know who owns the impressive mansions along Piccadilly near Monty and Lucy's house. Then there are the mansions that back up to Green Park and some of the older ones in the Whitehall area. Have I missed any?"

"That's most of them," Charles said.

"We need to start making inquiries, and the clubs will be a good place to begin," Devere said.

Georgiana peered again at her parchment. "We have only been able to rule out Lord Rhonson because his wife is ugly."

"I didn't say his wife is ugly," Caroline protested. "I merely said no one would think her a beauty."

"Same thing." Devere's gaze returned to the parchment. "We've got the Duke of Dorchester, the Duke of Harkey, and the Marquess of Williers. This should be easy. How should we go about this?"

It was a comfort to Charles that he would not be shouldering this responsibility alone, that Devere was eager to help. "What we really want to know is which of them is married to a remarkable beauty, but we can't just go around directly asking this because we can't risk reports of our inquisitiveness getting back to the husband or his evil wife. Our first concern is protecting Georgiana."

"I agree," Devere said. "There are more subtle ways of inquiring."

"For instance," Georgiana said, "one could say something like *Is that the one with the stunning wife?* Or *I wonder if his wife is the one who grew up with my mother.*"

"If you don't come across someone who knows the husband," Caroline suggested, "you might just try to find out where they live. Then we could have the house watched around the clock to confirm if the beautiful murderess lives there."

"You know, instead of Brook's, I believe I'll go to White's tonight," Devere offered. "First, I'll run by and grab Rockingham. He knows many more people than I because of all the work he's done for the government."

"I'd be very grateful," Charles said.

"If you find out anything," Georgiana said, "please let us know at once—no matter what time it is."

IT WAS A bitter disappointment to Georgiana that they heard not a single word from Devere last night. Obviously, he'd not learned anything that could reveal the identity of the man now married to Sarah Powell.

Georgiana must try to get her mind off the possibility she might be the target of a murder plot. Today she would concentrate on transforming her bedchamber. The painters had left, but the paint still hadn't dried. She wouldn't be selecting any new furnishings because she was pleased with what Charles's mother had chosen. She was only changing the color scheme. Once the paint dried, the linen draper would install new draperies, bed curtains, and bed coverings with the fabrics Georgiana had selected before their journey to Devon.

She intended to keep the handful of family portraits that hung in the chamber. Her favorite was a small one of Charles as a wee lad dressed in a long dress. He'd been such a lovely child.

All she needed now were accessories for the Carrara marble mantlepiece. The clock his mother had there lacked the elegance Georgiana wished to achieve. She wanted to feature a pair of Sevres vases in a bright pink. Since French imports were still difficult to get one's hands on, she thought her best course for obtaining the kind of vases she had in mind would be at one of Mr. Christie's sales. She knew she would have to go there in person. It would be impossible to tell the color from a catalogue.

Over breakfast, she shared her plan with Charles.

He grimaced. "So I'm to spend the day looking at items from dead people's houses?"

"Yes, my dearest. Unless you'd permit me to go with my sister or cousins. I'm sure they would love to go."

He shook his head. "I'm not taking my eyes off you."

At that very moment, her heart felt as if it overflowed with love for this man. She wanted to tell him how much she loved him, but she was too proud to do it. If he would only tell her he loved her, then she would feel like proclaiming her love for him from the spire of Westminster Abbey.

Could any woman have a better husband than she had? She'd never harbored the least doubt or slightest regret over their impetuous marriage, and everything that had occurred since only reinforced the depths of her love for him and her conviction that no man could have been a finer husband.

That he put her above all else indicated his high regard for her. His every touch told her how thoroughly he desired her. She didn't have to hear him declare his love. She felt it.

After breakfast, she left her seat and moved to him, pressing her lips to his cheek. "I'm very fortunate to have you for my husband."

The door suddenly opened, and there stood Devere.

CHAPTER EIGHTEEN

G EORGIANA LOOKED HOPEFULLY at her cousin. "Did you learn something at White's last night?"

"Not really, but I wanted to tell you the little bit I did learn."

He sat where Charles indicated, but he declined Georgiana's offer of a cup of tea. "I thought it best that I inquire about just one of the titled men at a time."

"Good decision," Charles said.

"So I started with the Marquess of Williers. I sat at a table with five men I've served with in the House of Lords and casually asked, *Say, do any of you know why Lord Williers doesn't take his seat?* Four of the men—who were younger, like me—did not know him, but Lord Simpson said something to the effect that he casually knew the fellow but couldn't answer why he had no interest in the House of Lords."

Charles's interest seemed to perk. "Simpson's quite a bit older than us."

"Yes, he is."

"So then?" Charles asked.

"I said it was understandable if one chose not to come to London, and that was when Lord Simpson told me that Williers spent a goodly amount of time in London, that he'd actually been at White's at least once in the past week.

"I didn't want to seem too inquisitive, but I said, *I've heard he's enormously wealthy. I suppose he lives in one of those huge mansions on Piccadilly*—which I knew to be untrue, seeing as I know every house on Piccadilly. That's when he told me Lord Williers lives in one of the old mansions built in Tudor times along the Thames not far from Whitehall."

Georgiana clapped her hands. "I think you've been quite successful. Now we simply spy on the Thames-side mansion to see what Lord Williers's wife looks like."

Devere shrugged. "It's a start."

"If this doesn't meet with success, we'll move on to one of the dukes," Charles said. He stood. "First off, I'm going send my groom over to Whitehall to find out exactly which house belongs to Lord Williers, then Georgiana and I will go observe."

"You can't let Georgiana near that place!"

"I assure you, she won't be seen. We'll be seated in an un-marked coach across the street."

Devere looked relieved. "If you need it, you're welcome to borrow the traveling coach my servants use. It's unmarked."

"Thank you. I will take you up on the offer."

"And I will begin to make inquiries about the dukes," Devere said.

BY THAT AFTERNOON, Charles's groom had returned from Whitehall and given his master the address of Lord Villiers. Charles gave him a shilling and told him not to mention to anyone the nature of today's inquiry. He trusted the boy—not that Jimmy was a boy anymore. He must be nearing twenty now. Charles then sent him to Devere House to collect the servants' coach. "You'll be our coachman today," he told the lad, whose face brightened at the prospect of driving the coach.

Later, as they were being driven to Whitehall, Georgiana cast a remorseful glance at her husband. "I feel like I'm such a burden. You can't enjoy anything because you're tied to me."

"And that's supposed to be a hardship? There's no one I'd rather spend time with than you."

A gentle smile on her face, her lashes lowered. "I want to tell you something I haven't actually owned up to before." She still wasn't looking at him.

She sounded so serious it frightened him. Had she done something she was ashamed to admit? Did she regret their marriage? His gut plummeted. "What is it?"

She swallowed. "I'm very happy that I married you. I love being married. I love everything about being married." Now she looked up at him. "Especially to you."

It was as if she were reaching into his own heart, expressing what he felt for this remarkable woman he'd wed. Could any man experience greater joy than her words had just brought him? He knew they were well suited. He knew they were sexually compatible. But he'd only hoped that this marriage could bring her a portion of the joy it had brought him.

Her declaration was like a gift from the gods. *She* was a gift from the gods. He'd been sitting across the carriage seat, but now he moved to sit beside her and draw her into his arms. He held her closely, murmuring into her ear. "Seeing you that day on Piccadilly was the luckiest day of my life."

She raised her face to his. "Mine, too."

His lips settled on hers for a hungry kiss.

Soon the coach stopped on Lord Williers' street. Charles had told his groom to park across the street from the house he'd located earlier. He'd also told Georgiana when they reached their destination, he'd sit opposite her so each of them would be able to ease open their respective velvet curtains enough to peer at the Williers' house.

With one last brush of his lips across his wife's cheek, he returned to the seat across from her.

Each of them moved the curtain only a sliver, and they peered at the tall, old brick house that was twice as large as Charles's house. Its pedimented white door relieved the building's brownish-red brick and was reached by three steps. He kept his eye on that white door.

"It's obvious they're in town," she said. "All the curtains at all the windows have been drawn open."

"Yes, that is fortuitous."

"You don't have to keep watch. I'll alert you if there's anything to see."

He shrugged. "What else would I do?"

"I suppose you should have brought all those newspapers from when we were gone to Devon so you could catch up on what occurred in Parliament while you were away from London."

"That is a good suggestion. If we're not successful today, I'll do that tomorrow."

"Though the light's not terribly good for reading inside the coach." She kept her eye on the slit of window curtain while talking.

"Ah, but your husband is possessed of excellent vision."

"Just another of your exceptional features," she said with a smile.

They continued to watch the house for a considerable period of time, but no one came, no one left. "My arm's getting sore from lifting this curtain," she eventually said. "How long have we been sitting here?"

He consulted his watch. "We arrived at eleven. It's now twelve thirty. No wonder your arm's sore."

"It should be time for the paying of calls."

"Yes. I would expect Lady Williers to either be hosting visitors today or visiting others. Care to wager which she'll be doing?"

"I rarely wager. I'm terrible at it."

Unfortunately, it proved to be the day Lady Willers received callers. At one o'clock a pair of women he took to be a mother and daughter arrived in an unmarked coach and were soon admitted.

"How old would you say the mother is?" Georgiana asked. "I suppose that was a mother and daughter duo."

"That would be my guess. The daughter was certainly no debutante. She had to be nearing thirty."

"That's what I thought."

"And the mother must be fifty."

Georgiana nodded.

A half hour later, the two women left the house.

Time was dragging by slower than frozen honey. How many days would they have to do this? He would do as Georgiana suggested and bring his stack of newspapers next time. If there were a next time.

No other callers came. He hoped Lady Williers would leave.

"How will we know if a solo woman leaving the house is Lady Willers?" she asked.

"We won't with certainty, but I have an idea."

For a second, she removed her gaze from the window and eyed him, her brows lifted in query.

"We follow. And when she stops, I'll go ask if she's Lady Willers."

"And how would you explain such curiosity?"

He thought for a moment. "I'll have to tell a white lie."

"Such as?"

"I'll say I've been told that Lady Williers bears a strong re-semblance to my . . . my aunt. That's how I identified her. And I'll say that the resemblance is remarkable."

"Will you use your real name?"

"No. I may use Freddie's."

Hour after hour went by, and no one else came to Willers House, no one else left Willers House. After they'd been sitting there five hours, they lost their sun when dusk fell. Still they sat in the coach until total darkness surrounded them.

"Come, love, you need a good dinner," he said. "We'll return tomorrow. And I'll bring my newspapers."

THE FOLLOWING DAY they arrived in front of the Willers' house at eleven. This time her husband did bring his stack of yellowing newspapers. As boring as the previous day had been, she still looked upon it as another one of the happiest days in her life. Charles had told her he preferred being with her over everything else.

She'd been totally stunned. It was almost inconceivable that he could feel toward her as powerfully as she felt toward him. She would not have dreamed on the day of their marriage that this bonding between them could come so much earlier than she'd thought possible.

One day she would confess how she'd fallen in love with him the afternoon they met, but she wasn't ready to expose her innermost emotions. Yet. But he must know how thoroughly she craved him. His every touch was a powerful aphrodisiac. She knew he found their lovemaking as sublime as she did. And that was just one facet of their complete unity.

To spare her aching arm, this time she brought a small box to sit on her lap to prop up her elbow while she tugged at the curtain. She carefully watched that white front door of Williers House. Noon came, but no visitors. No residents left.

At one o'clock, a crested coach drew up at the front of Williers House, and the coachman hopped off the box.

Georgiana's hopes fell. More visitors.

But no one left the coach. "A coach has drawn up to the door," she told her husband.

A moment later, the house's front door opened. Georgiana's heartbeat accelerated. A lone woman came out.

Disappointment coursed through her. The woman, who was nearing forty, was *not* Sarah Powell. From the quality of her impeccable clothing, Georgiana thought it was likely this was the wealthy Lady Williers. "A lone woman has left the house."

"For the purpose of elimination, I must find out if it's Mrs. Williers," Charles said. "Scoot over to the far side of the carriage." Once she did, he left the coach and walked across the street.

CHAPTER NINETEEN

After the fine carriage drove off, Charles returned to their borrowed coach and gave instructions to Jimmy before climbing into the coach, his face inscrutable.

"That was Lady Williers, was it not?" she asked, her voice revealing her disappointment.

He nodded solemnly, then with a mischievous glint in his eye, added, "Freddie Fortescue, at your service, my lady."

Even though she was discouraged, a choked giggle broke. She loved that he could make her laugh even at a time like this. "So you told her she resembled your aunt and that you were Freddie?"

"I did."

She settled back in her seat. "What next?"

"Hopefully Devere will have learned where the dukes live."

"Everything takes so long."

"At least your bedchamber's coming along nicely."

"I was happy to see the linen drapers arrive today. I expect by tonight, my chamber will be almost complete."

"We'll go to Mr. Christie's now and look for the last acquisition for my lady's chamber, that French porcelain." He moved closer and nibbled at her neck as he whispered. "Perhaps tonight we'll make love in your new bedchamber."

Her hand caressed his thigh. "That would be lovely."

>>>><<<<

THEIR AFTERNOON PASSED much more quickly than the hours they had spent waiting in vain in front of Williers House. When they visited Devere and told him Lady Williers was not the beautiful murderess, he vowed to do everything he could to find out where the dukes lived. "I will do my best to have that information by tomorrow morning," he'd told them.

At Mr. Christie's, the proprietor himself located a pair of Sevres vases that were even more beautiful than Georgiana had thought obtainable.

When they returned home at dusk, Freddie was waiting. "Come into the library, my good man," Charles said. The three of them settled in front of the fire, each clutching a glass of Madeira.

"I wanted to tell you, old boy," Freddie began, "I've been doing some sleuthing of my own. Seeing that you can't leave the wife, I thought to be your eyes and ears."

"That's very thoughtful of you," Charles said.

Though Georgiana did not know her husband's friend well, his speech pattern seemed to indicate a man deep in his cups. In fact, it seemed to her that every time she saw Freddie Fortescue, he spoke like one who'd imbibed too many drinks of strong spirits.

"Pray, enlighten us."

"I thought of Lady Churston's rejected suitors—from when she was Miss Beresford, of course—and I believe we need to eliminate all of them from suspicion."

"But we no longer believe they're responsible for the slanderous things the *Gazette* is printing about my wife."

Freddie frowned. "What a pity."

Her husband looked apprehensively at his friend. "What have you done, Freddie?"

"I knew you'd eliminated Sir Thomas and that Cunningham chap. Thought I might just try to bluff Aldridge, seeing as we're old friends with him."

"Good lord! What did you say to him?" Charles asked.

"Seeing as he's so disgustingly wealthy, I thought it possible he might have paid the crook who publishes the *Gazette*. So I said I'd heard that he'd paid a certain newspaper to print something about a certain lady."

"And what did he say to that?" Charles asked.

"Didn't say a thing for a moment. Acted mightily suspicious. But I wasn't about to let up when I felt I had a boot to his neck, so to speak."

"Please say you didn't mention my name," Georgiana said.

Freddie vigorously shook his head. "Nothing more than *a certain lady*."

"What exactly did you say to him?" Charles demanded.

"I told him *a certain lady* would be expecting a retraction, or all would be exposed. Might ruin his Parliamentary prospects."

"Not to mention his upcoming marriage," Charles said with a frown. "What was Aldridge's reaction?"

"Said the retraction would be in the morning paper."

THE FOLLOWING MORNING, Charles instructed the footman to rush out and buy that morning's *Gazette*. It seemed inconceivable to him that Aldridge could have been behind the scandalous attacks on Georgiana, especially given their suspicions about Sarah Powell.

Even before the footman returned with the paper, Freddie showed up, a dejected look on his face, as he handed the *Gazette* to his friend. "It ain't here."

Charles scanned the first page of the *Gazette*, his wife looking over his shoulder, but there was no kind of retraction, no mention of Georgiana. Charles proceeded to scan every subsequent page, but no retraction of any sort was printed. He shrugged his shoulders and tossed down the newspaper.

Charles looked up at his friend. "Perhaps tomorrow."

"Likely wasn't time after I met with Aldridge late yesterday. Expect it in tomorrow's edition." Freddy went from glum to hopeful. "I'm going to continue sleuthing for my best mate. I'm determined now to find that beautiful woman who burned up her husband." Then he took his leave.

After he was gone, Georgiana said, "I believe that's the first time I've seen Mr. Fortescue sober."

Charles chuckled. "That's the first time I've seen him rise before noon."

He and Georgiana then sat at the breakfast table where he began to peruse his newspaper of choice, *The Morning Chronicle*. To his surprise, a retraction appeared on its front page.

Actress Retains House on Bayswater Road

The *Chronicle* regrets that an account last week erroneously reported that a fine house belonging to a famed actress, S. R., had reverted to the bank. Contrary to the previous report, it seems the beauty's protector, one Lord A., has ensured the title to the house will be retained by S.R. in perpetuity.

Charles started to laugh, a deep, bellowing guffaw.

"What is so funny, dearest?"

"Poor Freddie. Poor Aldridge. There appears to have been a misunderstanding. Look at this." He handed her the newspaper.

Her mouth gaped open after she read the retraction. "You think Freddie and Lord Aldridge were talking of two different 'a certain lady' accounts?"

"I do, indeed. I knew Aldridge was planning to marry Lady Elizabeth Finley. That's why I discounted him of being vindicative toward you. Apparently, in preparation for his marriage, he was severing ties with the actress who's been his mistress the past two years."

"Oh, my! So he assumed Freddie was going to expose the

mistress if Lord Aldridge did not relent and restore the house to her?"

"Yes. I'd feel a great deal worse if Aldridge weren't so disgustingly well off financially. Though purchasing that house as a parting gift to one's mistress is extravagant, even for a wealthy man."

She started to laugh, too.

Devere entered the chamber. "It's good to see you two in such good humor. Considering."

Georgiana whirled around to face him. "We're not really, my dear cousin. Please tell me you've discovered another address for us. We seem to be spinning wheels that go nowhere."

Devere came and sat next to Georgiana on the sofa. "I had no luck with the Duke of Harkey, but I learned where the Duke of Dorchester resides."

"Where?" Georgiana asked.

"On Portman Square."

"I can't believe I didn't know that," Charles said.

"I believe the reason we're not acquainted with the duke—other than him not serving in Parliament—is that he's said to enjoy traveling and isn't often in London. Now that I'm thinking about it, I seem to recall in one of her letters, Sophia telling me she'd met the duke in Vienna a few months back."

Georgiana thought aloud. "I wonder if he's now returned to London."

Her cousin shrugged. "My contact—Lord Pembroke—didn't know for sure but thought he had returned from Vienna."

"Parliament does seem to be the glue that holds us aristocrats together," Charles said. "There are a rare few who don't serve, and, of course, those are the ones we don't know."

"So, will you two be sitting in our old coach today, spying at Portland Square?"

"Of course. Thank you again for the loan of your carriage," Georgiana said as her cousin stood.

"It won't be long before I have the address of the Duke of Harkey. I've only just remembered he's something high in the

Foreign Office. I've got contacts there who can let me know where he lives."

"How could I have not known that about him?" Charles asked.

"Because the man's nearer the age of your father. Not of our generation." Devere then bid them farewell.

＊＊＊＊＊

THAT AFTERNOON, ONCE again, Lord and Lady Churston sat in the unmarked coach across the street from the Duke of Dorchester's fine home on Portman Square. Constructed of large white stone, its stately lines had been inspired by classicism. It was without question the grandest house there, owing as much to its architect as it did to pristine maintenance.

Each of the rows of windows gleamed without a speck of dust. And, thankfully, draperies were drawn open at each of them. The Dorchesters must be in London.

Her husband had told her Portman Square and its fine houses had been built when his father was a young man, but any observer would think Dorchester House newly constructed. The shiny black paint at the door, the pair of gleaming brass lanterns flanking it, and the well-manicured pot plants spaced at even intervals in front of the symmetrical house all looked as if they had just been added to finish off the architect's seminal creation.

As Georgiana peered at Dorchester House, her husband unfolded a newspaper. He had once again brought more of the newspapers that had come out during the week they'd spent going to Devon. "In an hour or two, I'll be caught up on all that occurred while we were traipsing about the West Country."

"Did you miss anything important?" she asked.

"Not really."

She recalled him telling her nothing was more important to him than her. The very notion that he would not leave her side until the former Sarah Powell was locked away gave Georgiana an indelible sense of security. And joy.

"Darling?" she said.

He looked at her over the top of the newspaper, raising his brows.

"How did you like the transformation of my bedchamber? You didn't tell me last night, as you were . . . otherwise engaged." When she recalled her husband's amorous attentions, it was impossible to suppress a smile.

"The room has never looked lovelier. It's difficult to even remember that it used to be my mother's bland chamber."

"What did you like best?"

"Other than the bed?"

She shared a smile with him. "Other than *our* bed."

He thought a moment before answering. "I like that it reflects your personality. I believe if I saw a hundred different chambers, I could have seen your stamp on this one."

"My stamp? Pray, explain yourself."

"Well, the color. Pink suits you. But more than that, the lack of artifice, lack of extravagance, the simplicity of its loveliness is just like you."

Once again, she was struck by the affection in his voice and in his choice of words. She believed her dearest Charles must love her. To others, it might be a puzzle that two strangers could fall in love in so short a time. It might seem inconceivable that two people could come to understand each other so thoroughly in only a few weeks. But she and Charles were living proof that it was possible.

She might not be able to enumerate his lifelong friends or trace his family tree, but she knew that the choices he would make in life would always reflect dignity and duty and loyalty. She knew he was possessed of a kind heart. And she knew he was guided by the highest principles.

A crested carriage came to a stop in front of the Dorchesters'. "Dearest, do you recognize that crest?"

He put his newspaper down and slightly lifted away a corner

of the velvet curtain. "I believe that belongs to Lord Rickman."

"You know Lord Rickman?"

"Only by sight. He's a good bit older than I."

They watched as a lone woman swathed in an ermine-trimmed cape and carrying a huge, luxurious ermine muff trotted up the steps to Dorchester House. "The woman dresses very well," she said. "Like Sarah Whatever-Her-New-Name-Is."

"Perhaps they go to the same modiste."

Her heartbeat raced. Was Sarah Powell now the Duchess of Dorchester?

Georgiana intently watched the house. A half hour later, the well-dressed woman she presumed to be Lady Rickman left.

Between then and nightfall, no one else came or went from Dorchester House. It was difficult for Georgiana to conceal her disappointment when she knew they had to return home. Another unproductive day wasted.

"I have a better idea," Charles said.

"We are in need of a better idea," she said with a forced laugh.

"I'll have Jimmy make our inquiries."

"What inquiries?"

"He can go to the back door and ask the servants to describe their mistress. If the woman's as beautiful as everyone says Sarah Powell was, it will be obvious from the description of her. If they don't use the word beautiful, it can't be our quarry."

"And why is he going to be asking for her description?"

"I'll have him say he witnessed a finely dressed woman drop her reticule on Oxford Street, and if their description of the woman he saw matches theirs, he will return the reticule to their mistress. Of course, I'll tell Jimmy what the woman we seek looks like. Then he can make up a description that bears no resemblance to her or to the Duchess of Dorchester—once they tell him what their mistress looks like."

"Oh, my darling, that is brilliant!"

"I'll have Jimmy go around now—after we move this coach to the next street."

CHAPTER TWENTY

AFTER JIMMY MOVED the coach to the next street, Charles and Georgiana awaited in its near-total darkness. "What's your guess about what Jimmy will learn?" he asked his wife.

"I'm terrible at guessing, but I have a feeling our evil woman just may be the Duchess of Dorchester."

"And what's contributed to that opinion?"

"The house is so very tasteful. The visitor was dressed so beautifully. Because of how exquisite the she-devil looked that day on Piccadilly, I can see her as mistress of that beautiful mansion."

"That makes sense." If the woman they sought proved to be the Duchess of Dorchester, what should his next step be?

Jimmy returned, and Charles threw open the carriage door. "Well?"

"The Duchess of Dorchester ain't your woman. The cook I spoke with said the duchess be 'bout forty with graying hair."

Charles sighed. "Thank you for trying, Jimmy. We'll return home now."

Jimmy closed the coach door.

"It must be the Duchess of Harkey then," Georgiana said.

"Unless your Sarah Powell took another Christian name."

"In which case, we will be forced to start all over."

"And may never find the former Sarah Powell."

"Don't say that. It may take a while, but someone in the Capital is bound to know of an aristocrat who's so incredibly beautiful."

When they arrived home, a note from Devere awaited them. Wordlessly, Charles unfolded it. After reading it, he looked up at his viscountess. "It's the address of the Duke of Harkey . . . and the Harkeys are in London."

"Hopefully," Georgiana said, "tomorrow we'll know for sure. So, to spare us the most boring task in the three kingdoms tomorrow, will you send Jimmy to make inquiries of the servants as to the appearance of their mistress?"

"I've been thinking about that . . ."

"And?"

"I'm going myself."

"No! Those people are murderers! That's much too dangerous. You might be recognized. You are, after all, a member of Parliament."

He chuckled. "I won't go as myself."

Her brows drew together. "Then who?"

"I shall borrow clothing that belongs to my coachman."

"You're going to pretend to be a coachman?" She could not conceal her smile.

"Who better to do the job? Little as I like to leave you, this way I can ensure control of exactly what's said. I'll say the duchess's coach rushed off, and I wasn't able to return the dropped reticule to her. Then I'll ask for verification of her description. I'll even take one of your reticules in order to be convincing."

"You're certainly convincing me."

He leaned down and kissed her. "Come along to the dining room. I'm famished."

Not wanting to be seen leaving his house dressed shabbily, at noon the next day Charles left the rear door of his house and at the mews, climbed upstairs to the quarters where the grooms and coachman slept.

"I've a big favor to ask of you, Childers," he said to his coachman. He'd selected Childers because the coachman was the only servant who was as tall as Charles. Unfortunately, Childers was quite a bit heavier, but hopefully Charles would be able to keep the breeches from falling down.

"I could never deny you nothing, my lord."

"I'm afraid I'm going to have to borrow the clothes you're wearing."

A shocked look on his face, Childers said, "Are you joking me, my lord?"

"No, I'm serious. We shall trade clothing. I need to appear to be a coachman, but it will only be for a short time. I'll restore your clothing to you in about an hour."

"Certainly, my lord." Childers began to remove his clothes.

Within fifteen minutes, Charles was knocking at the back door of Harkey House. A man dressed as a footman answered it, his skeptical gaze going from Charles's face to the gloved hand holding a woman's costly reticule. His brow lifted in query.

"Someone told me," Charles began, "that the lovely woman who dropped this 'ere reticule on Oxford Street might be the Duchess of Harkey. I wanted to restore it to 'er, but I needs to be reassured this really belongs to your duchess. Can you do me the goodness of describing yer mistress?"

The footman thought for a moment before answering. "The Duchess of Harkey is about thirty years of age and of average height. Her hair is black."

All of those fit Sarah Powell, but why in the devil had the fellow not mentioned her beauty? Charles cleared his throat. "So the duke ain't married to a beauty?"

"I wouldn't say that. No. I just don't feel right saying as how my mistress is . . . well, beautiful."

Charles nodded. "Then that ain't the woman I saw on Oxford Street. That woman what dropped this 'ere reticule did have black hair, but her face looked like a 'orse, if ye know what I mean." Tipping his hat, Charles thanked the man and left.

His mind whirled with plans as he rode a saddlehorse back to Berkeley Square. The more he thought about the duchess's premeditated murders, the more convinced he became that she had not acted alone. She and the duke must have concocted the scheme. Who else could have been on hand that night to whisk her away from the burning house?

Charles was determined that the pair of them would pay for their crimes. He would discuss with Devere how they would proceed to seek justice.

Before he talked with Devere, though, he needed to tell Georgiana that they had finally found their woman.

In the coachman's quarters, he dressed in his own clothing, then entered the back door of his house.

And met with chaos.

The cook was weeping, "Oh, my lord, it's awful."

"What's awful?" Had she burnt the mutton?

"It's Jonathan . . ." She started sobbing before she could finish. "He's been stabbed."

Had Charles himself been stabbed, he could not have experienced a greater fear. *Georgiana!* "My wife!" He rushed down the central corridor through splatters of blood. He raced up the bloody stairs, his heartbeat roaring, his entire body trembling.

Georgiana's hysterical maid met him at the top of the stairs. Between anguished cries, she said. "They've taken her!"

CHAPTER TWENTY-ONE

C HARLES'S FIRST INSTINCT was to race after her, but he had no idea where she'd been taken. He needed to learn more. *"They?* Tell me everything."

"You'd best talk to Jonathan."

"I thought he'd been stabbed."

"He was, but thank the Lord he wasn't killed."

Killed. Charles was horribly afraid Georgiana would meet such a fate. His gaze shifted along the corridor, following the splatters of blood. "Where is he?"

"Mrs. Jones is tending to his wound. I hope you don't object that they've put him on yer bed, my lord."

Charles rushed to his bedchamber, following a trail of blood. His housekeeper was bending over the bed where the youthful footman's lanky body stretched. His crimson-stained shirt crumpled on the floor. Mrs. Jones was staunching the bleeding from a gash in Jonathan's bony ribcage.

Charles felt as powerless as a crippled nag. "Have you sent for a surgeon?"

Mrs. Jones nodded. "Wilcox has gone." She continued pressing down on the wound with a pad of linen sheeting.

Charles moved closer to the bed and spoke to the injured footman. "What happened?"

"I'm so sorry, my lord," Jonathan said in a weakened voice. "I tried to keep those men from entering the house. I tried to protect Lady Churston, but one of them stabbed me."

"Thank God you weren't killed. I'm very sorry you were injured, and I'm very much in your debt. Were you able to observe what happened next?"

Jonathan shook his head ruefully. "I lost consciousness and fell to the floor." The injured footman looked at the housekeeper, who took up the tale.

"The men came racing up the stairs, throwing open the doors to every chamber," Mrs. Jones said. "They were looking for both you and Lady Churston."

If only he'd been here. "How many were there?"

"Three."

"And they got my wife?"

Her eyes filled with tears, she nodded. "She was screaming and kicking as two of them dragged her from her bedchamber." Her voice broke. "She was . . . she was calling for you."

It was all he could do not to bawl like a woman. "Did they . . . hurt her?"

"I don't think so, other than rough handling her wrists. Her ladyship's maid tried to help her, but they struck her, knocking her against a wall. I think she, too, has suffered some injuries."

His staff had behaved admirably. He had no one to blame but himself. He should never have left. He had known what kind of evil the Harkeys were capable of. From the moment he'd left Piddletown, he'd known the potential threat against his wife's life. She was the only person in London who could identify the former Sarah Powell, the only one in London who knew about those two burned bodies back in Manston Stoney.

His lips folded into a grim line. He was nearly overcome with the sick, oppressive crush of dread. *She would be killed.* "Did anyone see what kind of vehicle they took her away in?"

"I did, my lord," Mrs. Jones said calmly, looking up from her patient to eye her employer. "I peeked out the front window and saw those horrid men force her into a traveling coach."

"How many horses?" He hoped to God not more than two.

"Four."

His already-churning gut plummeted. That meant they would likely be traveling away from London. How in the hell was he to find her? "Tell me anything you can about what these men looked like and anything you can about the coach." He was hoping she would confirm his belief that the Duke of Harkey was just as involved in these evil schemes as his loathsome wife.

Thank God his housekeeper had kept a clear head. She drew a deep breath. "All three men were dressed shabbily. One was older—about fifty, I'd say. His hair was solid gray, and he was giving orders. The two others were younger, probably in their middle twenties. None of them spoke like a gentleman."

Now he knew the duke was not directly involved in the abduction, as Charles initially suspected. Still, Charles believed the duke was orchestrating it along with the murderous former Mrs. Powell. "Were the men armed?"

"I couldn't say. We know at least one of them had a knife." She glanced at Jonathan.

"I believe they all had knives," Jonathan said.

"As to the coach," Mrs. Jones continued, "it looked as if it had once been grand. In fact, it appeared a crest had been painted over."

That the men hadn't just killed Georgiana outright told Charles they had a reason for keeping her alive, and he knew what that reason was. They had to find out how many others his wife had told of the murders in Manston Stoney.

Gripped by a choking sense of despair, he knew finding Georgiana was as likely as the Reverend Powell rising from the grave. Yet find her he must. Right now, Georgiana was the victim of an abduction. He must locate her before she was the victim of a murder. And there was nothing he wouldn't do to save his wife.

MINUTES LATER, ARMED with sword, musket, and knife sheathed in his boot, Charles rounded the corner to pound on the door of Devere House. As determined as Charles was to save his wife and as willing as he was to lay down his life to do so, he knew that a single man could not prevail against three or more armed men.

His wife's cousin came rushing to him. "What's the matter?"

"They've taken Georgiana! We've got to find her." He proceeded to relate the details of her abduction.

"You think it's the Duke and Duchess of Harkey?"

"I think they're behind the abduction. Yes."

"How in the devil will we find her?"

"We start at Harkey House."

"They won't be keeping her there."

"I know that! But I'm betting that she-devil's there, and if they're threatening to kill my wife, I can threaten to kill his wife." His voice cracking, he added, "If they hurt Georgiana, I swear I'll kill that woman!"

Devere winced. "We need all the help we can get. I'll send notes around to Rockingham and Monty to have them meet us at Harkey House."

"Specify that they come armed."

"I will." He jotted two notes. "It will just take me a minute to arm myself."

That minute and the five minutes they had to wait while Devere's horse was saddled seemed like five hours to Charles. Every second counted. Georgiana could be killed at any moment. A paralyzing, sickening dread soaked into every crevice of the sponge his insides had become.

Once they were astride their horses and racing to Kensington, with every clop of his horse's hooves, he prayed they would find Georgiana in time. It was several minutes more until they drew near the sprawling, multi-chimney mansion of the Harkeys.

"Are we going to the front?" Devere asked.

"Because we're armed, they might not open the door to us. Our luck might be better at the back door." It still sickened

Charles that his foray earlier today to the back of Harkey House might have cost his wife's life. Fear cascaded through him like a waterfall.

They rode to the rear of Harkey House and tried to enter the door, but it was locked. "You knock," he instructed Devere. Even though Charles was dressed vastly differently than he had been an hour earlier, he thought it best that Devere's face was the first one seen by whoever answered the door.

"We'll push our way in, swords drawn," Charles said.

They dismounted, and Devere knocked as Charles tethered their horses.

As soon as the door was cracked open, Devere shoved his weight into it. Both men drew swords and rushed in.

The scullery maid who'd opened the door screamed like an injured rook. Two, then three, more servants rushed to the kitchen but backed away, arms raised, when they saw the swords.

"Where's the duke?" Charles demanded, eyeing a tall man of about thirty who looked to be a footman.

"He's gone to the country."

"And the duchess?"

"She's in her study."

The tip of Charles's rapier jabbed the man's gut. "Show me."

Still holding up his trembling hands, the footman led them through the corridor that was lined with Turkey carpet runners, then up a broad staircase of darkened old oak.

On the upstairs landing, the footman turned to the left and walked down a dark corridor. He came to stand in front of a closed door and went to knock.

"Don't," Charles said. He shoved aside the footman and swung open the door.

A lone woman sat at a French writing desk, facing a window, her back to them. Then she turned around.

There was no mistake. This had to be the former Sarah Powell, the current Duchess of Harkey. Hair as black as coal framed an unmistakably perfect face of smooth, pale skin, a thin, slightly aquiline nose, large sapphire eyes framed by long black lashes. He'd never seen a more exquisitely beautiful woman.

When she saw that he aimed his sword at her, her eyes widened, and her rosy mouth turned hard.

"You may be meeting your Maker, Sarah Powell."

CHAPTER TWENTY-TWO

T HIS WAS NOT an abduction. That Georgiana's captors had not blindfolded her told her they didn't care if she saw where she was being taken. She would never leave the destination. After she was so forcefully tossed into the battered old coach, one of her foul-smelling captors tied together her hands with rough, scratchy rope. That man then sat next to her.

The older man, who was missing both eye teeth, sat across from her, smirking as his lazy gaze traveled from the top of her head to her lap, lingering over her bosom. Would the loathsome man try to take liberties with her before her killed her?

As disgusting as that idea was, the will to live was stronger.

She knew, too, with a stab of overwhelming grief, that her husband was likely to meet the same, horrifying fate. These men had tried in vain to find him when they had stormed into their house. That must mean the Duke and Duchess of Harkey suspected that she'd revealed to Charles her suspicions about Sarah Powell's faked death.

She prayed that Charles could elude these vipers. She even held out a slim hope that by some miracle he would be able to find her and rescue her.

But finding her would not be easy. As she watched through the coach window, it became evident that she was being taken from London. They went west, past Hyde Park, past Holland

House, and an hour later, past Hounslow. They were now deep into Middlesex. She began to despair. Charles would never be able to find her.

As it grew darker and darker, it became increasingly more difficult for the coachman to see. A near total blackness surrounded the slowly plodding carriage. The farther away from London they went, the farther away they went from any signs of habitation. And the farther they went from any possible rescue.

Finally, light pecked at the distant horizon, and the coach lurched toward it like the needle on a compass. As they drew closer, the shape of a large country house sharpened. Several of its windows were lighted against the night sky.

The coach pulled up to its front door. Because of the magnificence of the house, she instinctively knew it must be one of the residences of the Duke of Harkey. Her growing conviction that the duke was just as culpable as his wife in the Manston Stoney murders was now solidified.

The horrid man who'd sat beside her forced her from the coach and slung her over his shoulder as if she were a rolled-up piece of carpet. She was taken through the candlelit entry of the old mansion and down a flight of backstairs to a musty basement and a small room lighted by a single candle. It must have been a storeroom at one time. There she was dropped to the floor. Her shoulder hurt. Her palms stung where she'd tried to block the fall. As the door was locked behind her, she slowly lifted her head from the wooden floor.

And she looked into the eyes of Freddie Fortescue.

"IF YOU DON'T want to meet the same fate as the late Reverend Powell," Charles said to Sarah, the Duchess of Harkey in a guttural voice, "you will tell me where Lady Churston's been taken."

"I don't know what you're talking about." The woman was as cool as a block of marble.

He moved closer, his gaze riveted to those huge blue eyes. She didn't even blink. He'd never thought to be face-to-face with such sheer evil. He didn't believe he would have any qualms about thrusting his rapier through her cold heart. Instead, it stabbed at her upper left arm, drawing blood.

She screamed out in pain, and the expression on her face changed from defiance to fear.

He had her now.

"Where is she?" he demanded again.

"You were supposed to be with her." Her voice was filled with dismay. "Before my husband permanently silences the pair of you, he needs to find out who else has learned of what occurred at the parsonage at Manston Stoney."

"I'll ask once more. The next time, I'll drive my sword through your right hand." Charles's gaze flicked to Devere. "Hold her down, won't you, Lord Devere?"

"No, please!" she begged. "I'll tell you. My husband meant to have the pair of you taken to our house in Middlesex. He planned to question you there. Before killing you."

Charles had to get there before he killed Georgiana. "See if you can find something with which to bind this woman's hands, feet, and mouth, Devere. We're taking her with us." Charles planned to use her life as a bargaining tool when he faced the evil Duke of Harkey.

One of the Harkey grooms agreed to lead them to the duke's Middlesex estate. Devere agreed to be responsible for getting the duchess there. He slung her over his horse in much the same way as a saddle, her belly straddling the horse, her arms to the horse's left, her legs to the right. Before Devere mounted the horse, he warned her that if she should happen to fall off, he would see to it that his horse trampled her. Then he mounted the horse.

Just as they were ready to depart Harkey House, Rockingham and Monty arrived, both men, like Charles, Beresfords through marriage. They were fully armed on saddle horses. As the four men and their captive set off for Middlesex, Devere apprised them of what was occurring.

Surely, Charles told himself, the duke wouldn't kill Georgiana until he was able to extract from her the information he sought. He hoped to God she could hold out until he got there.

CHAPTER TWENTY-THREE

G EORGIANA QUICKLY SAW that, like her, Freddie's hands were tied, his behind his back while hers were tied in front of her. "What are you doing here?" she asked.

"Regret to say my tongue got away with me."

"What do you mean?"

"Trying to help you. Made inquiries." He shrugged. "Apparently, the Duke of Harkey—a most nasty fellow—was in the next room and overheard me." A sorrowful look on his face, he confessed, "Regret to say I may not have been completely sober. Deepest apologies, my lady. Charles's going to kill me."

"I fear the Duke of Harkey will beat him to it."

He gave a morose nod. "Expect you're right. Least I can do is try to defend you."

"How can you do that when your hands are tied behind your back—and you've got no weapon."

"Got a weapon."

"What?"

He nodded. "In me boot. Always carry one. Might need to do battle with footpads, you know."

"Then we must do our best to get you out of that rope. Do you suppose I can reach into your boot and extract the knife?"

"We can try." He scooted closer, and she drew herself up to her knees and attempted to slither her bound hands into the small space between his boot and his calf bone. If her hands hadn't been forced to move together by being tied, she would have been able to fit a single hand into the space, but as it was, this wasn't working.

If only she could remove the rope from her hands. She tried forcing it over her hands, but it was tied too tightly. That explained why her wrists had been rubbed raw and bloody.

She tried another dozen times but met with no success.

"What about biting it?" he asked.

She was willing to give it a go. Several attempts at that resulted in nothing more than spitting out miniscule, rough fibers.

"Will you allow me to try?" he asked. "Perhaps my teeth are sharper than yours."

He bent his head and closed his teeth around the fat rope that bound her hands and chomped forcefully. Once. Twice. Three times.

But he met with no more success than she had.

"Any ideas for a new plan?" he asked, giving up.

"I'm thinking. We've got to do something. We can't depend on Charles to save us. There's no way he will ever learn where we've been taken."

Just then, the door burst open, and a well-dressed man of about fifty with a commanding air strode into the small room. Silver haired and slender, his patrician countenance left no doubt this man had been born to a dukedom. He came to stand next to Georgiana and glared down at her.

"Ah, the former Beresford girl who is incapable of keeping her suspicions to herself. I know you've told Mr. Fortescue here as well as your husband about that business with the fire back at Manston Stoney. Tell me, who else have you told?"

She need not be guided by the truth with this evil man. "The Beresfords are a large family. You can't kill all of us."

"If you think me stupid enough to believe that, you're even more stupid than you think I am."

She shrugged. "I honestly don't care what you believe. I

know only this: the Beresfords will see that you and your wicked wife pay for what you've done."

A malevolent look crossed his face—was it fear?—and he sneered at her. "I don't believe you."

"Suit yourself, Your Grace," she spat out.

"By tomorrow morning, I hope to have captured that husband of yours." A wicked flash fired his dark eyes as he looked from her to Freddie. "The three of you will die tomorrow."

She would far rather die alone than be the instrument of Charles's death. Her dear, beloved Charles. He would have been far better off if he'd never met her.

Just last week she'd thought that day on Piccadilly the luckiest of her life for it had brought her Charles. Now she rued that day, the day she'd set eyes on the beautiful, calculating, cold-hearted seductress and murderer, the current Duchess of Harkey.

THE ONLY THING Charles had to be thankful for was the lack of rain in recent days. Had these ill-maintained country roads been mired in mud, they would not have been able to travel through the moonless night. It was as dark as a cave.

Were he not so terrified over his wife being the target of a murderer, he might have thought more of his own discomfort in the frigid weather. He did regret not grabbing his great coat and a woolen muffler. At least he had thick, lined leather gloves, though his hands—like his neck and ears—still stung from the cold. The howling, chilled winds increased his misery, but physical misery was easier to bear than his worry over Georgiana.

Progress was incredibly slow. They'd left Harkey House two hours previous and had only reached Hounslow. He knew saddle horses were far faster than ancient carriages like the one in which his wife had been whisked away, but daylight would have cut that time in half. How long had it taken Georgiana to reach the house she was being taken to?

With each passing moment, his doubts increased, his worry mounted. Would he get there in time to save Georgiana? He had to.

As they rode through the night, they discussed what they would do when they reached their destination. "One thing needs to be clear," Charles said. "It's my wife, and it's my life that must be risked first."

"She's my cousin," Devere countered. "I'll not cower before that deranged duke."

"I appreciate each of you for joining me on this dangerous mission," Charles said. "I can't stress enough how much peril you may face. Those people have already murdered two innocents. It's imperative they pay for what they've done, but it's even more important that we save Georgiana."

He told them that two young and one old man had performed the abduction and that he knew the duke himself was supposed to be at the Middlesex property. "I know not if there will be more than those four men there. I do believe the three henchmen are skilled at knives."

More than another hour later, the Harkey groom pointed out the duke's mansion in the distance. The men dismounted and silently led their horses uphill to the hulking house. The squares that were its windows gave off a buttery glow that served as a beacon in the night's blackness.

A sick queasiness in his gut, Charles led the group, eating up the distance as quickly as he could. He must reach her before that madman . . . it was too painful to finish the thought.

CHAPTER TWENTY-FOUR

"IF THEY WOULD have just taken us to Harkey House," Freddie said, "I have every confidence Charles would have found us there."

"But there's no hope he'll come here."

"All my fault. I must try to save you."

"That's impossible"

"'Tis not! When he comes back—that vile duke, that is—I shall attack him with every ounce of strength I possess. (Even if I say so meself, I'm considered skilled at pugilism.) While he's fending me off, you must use the opportunity to escape this room. Give you my word, I'll hold him back."

She shook her head. "He won't come alone. There will be others to ensure their employer doesn't sustain injury."

Freddie frowned. "Suppose you're right. Like Charles—he's always right. Suppose that's one of the reasons he fell in love with you. In addition to you being pretty, you're wise, like him."

Charles in love with me? Could he have told his closest friend that? How silly she was to be contemplating if Charles was in love with her when she should be spending every second she had devising a way to get out of here. Alive. She cleared her throat. "Did Charles ever tell you he was in love with me?"

"Certainly."

Her heart leapt. "When would that have been?" she asked,

striving to sound casual.

"When he told me he meant to marry you. Said he thought he'd loved you ever since he clapped eyes on you at Eton when you were a mere girl. Did he not tell you about that love-at-first-sight thing?"

"No, he didn't."

"Well, the fellow's dotty over you. Been scared to death of losing you to the fiend duke. Hope you love Charles like he loves you. He deserves it."

"I do," she whispered. "I, too, believe in love at first sight."

"You fell in love with Charles at first sight?"

"Indeed I did. And I love him more every day."

"What a pity you won't be able to tell him that. He would like to have heard it." He shook his head erratically. "Forget what I just said. 'Course you'll get to tell him that yourself. I will see to it that you get out of this wretched place." His voice turned somber. "When you're reunited with your husband, you must tell him how sorry I was to have jeopardized you."

She knew poor Freddie intended to offer his own life to make amends. Any rancor she might have felt for him earlier now fell away like a half-forgotten dream upon awakening.

SINCE NONE OF the lighted windows had been on the first floor, Charles felt confident the duke, his henchmen, and Georgiana would all be on the next two levels.

His first clue that Harkey must not keep much of a staff here was the absence of lighted lanterns at the mansion's front door. It was almost a certainty that no footman or butler would be answering that door. Charles raced ahead of the others and tried the front door. It was locked.

Like a cat on soft paws, he began to circle the home and try the other ground-floor entrances, but each of them also proved to be locked. Because the house was so vast and because the inhabitants were likely to be on the upper floors, he decided to risk gaining entry by smashing the French windows that gave out to a rear terrace. He drove the butt of his musket into one of the panes and cringed at the crashing sound as the shards of glass cascaded to the floor. He prayed the sound wouldn't be heard on the upper floors.

The others gathered around. "We must find the duke first," Charles whispered harshly as he opened the door and moved into a dark room. As much as he wanted to save Georgiana, he knew that as long as the duke was free, her life was in danger.

"It would help if we knew what he looked like," Devere quipped.

"I know what Harkey looks like," Lord Rockingham said.

"So do I," Monty added.

"Good." Charles put index finger to his mouth and began to move into the dark chamber. That large room opened onto a broad entryway that was lighted by a wall sconce. Thank God it was warm. His shivering lessened.

Sword drawn, he then led the way as quietly as possible up the broad wooden stairway. Monty had slung the duchess over his shoulder, but she was far from compliant. Even though her feet were tied tightly at the ankles, she did her best to kick him and hit him, and even though her mouth was firmly bound, she still managed to emit shrill sounds that, thankfully, did not carry far.

To the right, the landing spilled into a vast drawing room, so Charles assumed the duke's private chambers would be to the left. He moved along the dimly lit corridor, his gaze fixed on a bar of light beneath one of the doors midway down.

He paused outside that door, his heartbeat exploding. He prayed the element of surprise would give him enough of an edge to prevail over the duke. He twisted the door handle and shoved it open.

An older man who had been sitting by the fire drinking a dark liquid, leapt to his feet, eyeing Charles with hostility. The very manner with which he held himself bespoke privilege and a life-long pattern of command.

"That's Harkey," Rockingham said.

Monty entered the carpeted chamber and set down the duchess.

The duke's sharp gaze moved to his duchess. "What have you done to my wife?"

"What have you done to *my* wife?" Charles countered. His sword gave Charles the advantage over the Duke of Harkey.

Like a dethroned king, the duke sagged back into his chair. His air of confidence deflated; it seemed he knew he'd been defeated.

Charles moved closer. "Where is Lady Churston?" What if she had already been killed? The very thought was like a blow to Charles's windpipe.

"She and Freddie Fortescue are behind a locked door in the basement."

"Where's the key?"

The duke reached into a slit in his silk brocade waistcoat, withdrew the key, and tossed it to Charles.

"Why Freddie?" Charles asked.

"He knew about what happened at Manston Stoney."

How had that been revealed? Never mind. Getting Georgiana was all that mattered right now.

Charles eyed Rockingham. "Stay here and guard the duke and duchess." Charles flew from the chamber and raced down the stairs.

Chapter Twenty-Five

I T WAS BAD enough that she was going to die. That she would be responsible for bringing about Freddie's and Charles's deaths was even more unbearable. Georgiana wished she'd never told her husband of her suspicions about the beautiful Sarah Powell. Then he would never have told Freddie, and neither would have asked any awkward questions that put them under suspicion. Had she stayed silent, she might have been able to spare the life of the man she loved with all her heart. But she was now fairly confident that eventually the Duke and Duchess of Harkey would have decided to permanently silence her by committing another murder.

Nothing could be done now to prevent her death. Every mile they had moved farther away from London in that odious coach had taken her farther away from any hope of being rescued.

At least she now had the contentment of knowing she possessed Charles's love.

"I'm sorry, Mr. Fortescue, for involving you in this wretched situation. I know your intentions were pure. You only meant to help us."

"What a pity. My well-intended help turned into a deadly hindrance."

"Don't blame yourself. They would have killed me regardless. I'm most horribly sorry you'll die because of me." Her insides crashed. "And Charles, too," she added in a choked voice as tears gathered in her eyes.

"Our candle's about to burn out," Freddie said solemnly.

The strike of footsteps on the wooden floorboards outside their chamber frightened her. Had the duke decided to take her life tonight? "Did you hear that?" she asked Freddie in a panicked voice.

He leapt to his feet and moved to the door. "Yes."

Dear Freddie still thought that his martyrdom might save her.

The scrape of a metal into the lock sent her pulse racing in fear.

The door flew open. There stood the most magnificent sight she'd ever seen. Her husband's hair had been tousled by the wind, and his cheeks were stained pink from the cold, neither of which could detract from his undeniable virility. He was the most appealing man she'd ever seen. Her gaze traveled from his booted feet planted in the doorway and up his long, muscled legs and along the torso to his significant shoulders. This was a man capable of beating whatever obstacles were thrown in his way. This was a man of unquestionable bravery. This was the man she loved.

Her husband gazed from Freddie to her. "Are you unhurt?" he asked her in a grave voice.

"I'm wonderful now." A smile cracked on his handsome face as he moved into the chamber and withdrew a knife from his own boot. He slashed away the ropes at her hands and feet, then moved to his friend and did the same.

"I'm beastly sorry, old fellow," Freddie began, but Charles cut him off.

"Go upstairs and see if Devere and the others need your help."

As Freddie left the chamber, the candle went completely out. She and Charles found each other in the dark, his arms closing tightly around her. It was as if by holding her so close he would never again lose her. Tears of joy streamed down her cheeks.

She had a thousand questions to ask, but all that mattered at this moment was being with Charles and knowing they were going to live. There would be time for answers later.

Where Charles was concerned, she would no longer let her foolish pride keep her from speaking. "When I thought I was going to die, one of my biggest regrets was not being completely honest with you," she whispered.

"I cannot believe you've ever lied to me."

"Not lies. I just neglected to tell you something very important."

"You were already married?" he teased.

"No!"

"What then?"

"I never told you that I experienced love at first sight—at first sight of you that fateful day on Piccadilly."

He continued to hold her close as he softly chuckled. "That makes two of us."

"I wish I had back those first few days of our marriage when we were both too proud to reveal to one another what was in our hearts."

"Don't regret a single moment of our marriage—and don't forget we have a lifetime stretching ahead of us. Now."

"Thanks to my brave and brilliant husband. How ever did you find us?"

"I'll tell you as we climb the stairs and join the others."

Hand in hand, they walked up the stairs, but as they reached the ground floor, it became obvious a fight was going on one floor up. Furniture crashed. Glass broke. Men winced and shouted and cursed. And she recognized the voice of at least one of the men who had forcefully taken her from her Berkeley Square bedchamber.

CHAPTER TWENTY-SIX

"**Y**OU STAY HERE!" Charles rasped. He unsheathed his knife and gave it to her. "Use this if one of them comes for you."

His sword drawn, he hurried to the duke's apartments. The men who'd arrived with Charles were struggling with ill-dressed men he presumed to be the ones who'd captured Georgiana. His group had the advantage because they fought with swords; the others wielded knives. Unfortunately, he feared those in his group could be killed if the knives were hurled at them.

Freddie stood in the corner, armed only with the small knife Charles knew he kept in his boot. Freddie's stricken gaze met his friend's.

"Get my musket," Charles ordered. "It's just outside that door."

Freddie sped from the chamber and returned immediately with the musket, which he directed at the Duke and Duchess of Dorchester.

The duke, whose arm hooked around his cowering duchess, did not appear to have a weapon.

Devere quickly got the best of his foe, who fell back and was grounded when Devere planted his boot on the fellow's chest, rapier point at his throat.

Charles had, in the meantime, moved toward the corner that

Rockingham was being backed into. He had to keep Rockingham from being stabbed. But as Charles turned, he felt a stab pierce his back. A starburst of pain exploded. Freddie, musket in hand, rushed to him and yanked the knife from between his ribcage and lower shoulder. Charles nearly lost consciousness from the pain, but he forced himself to whirl around and face whoever it was who'd tried to kill him.

The Duke of Harkey smirked.

Freddie tried to see to Charles's wound, but Charles shook him off. "Help Rockingham," Charles managed in a weakened voice as he staggered toward the duke. Even though his strength was draining away with every drop of blood gushing down his back, Charles was sizing up his competition. He was much larger than Harkey and more than twenty years younger.

It took all his strength to grip the hilt, but he somehow managed to lunge toward the duke. The now unarmed duke retreated. That was a foolish thing to do. A few more steps, and he'd be against the wall. Now Charles had the upper hand. He marched Harkey one step back, then two, and then a third. He could go no further. A panicked look swept over the duke's aging face.

Charles debated what to do next. He wanted to pin the vile man against the wall by catching his flesh with his sword, but his honor prevented him from harming an unarmed man. Never mind that Harkey had been armed a moment earlier when he'd slung his knife at Charles. While Charles was contemplating this, something jammed into the wound in his back.

He cried out in splintering pain and whirled around. His gaze caught sight of a bloody circle midway down the duchess's sleeve. The woman had rammed her elbow into his torn flesh! As he limped toward the evil duchess, Georgiana, apparently unable to stay where he'd left her, strode into the chamber, her eyes flashing with anger as she rushed to the woman who'd further injured her husband.

"How dare you try to harm my husband!" Directing the knife

he'd given her at the still-gagged duchess, she said, "Go stand next to your husband or I'll stab you with this knife, and I can promise you'll not walk away from that."

Charles didn't like his wife being in this room with all these evil, dangerous people, but he could not deny he admired her courage.

An explosive sound shattered the air, and he looked to see a puff of powder above the musket Freddie had just fired. The man who'd been fighting with Rockingham dropped to the ground. That the man was dead was obvious.

Charles's gaze then flicked to Monty, who towered over the opponent he was intimidating with his superior skill. A moment later, their last enemy was dropping his knife and begging to be spared.

Georgiana kept her head even though her tears poured. "We must send for a surgeon! Charles is hurt."

"I'll go," Freddie said.

"Do you know where to go?" Charles asked, an amused expression on his face.

"No, but I'll find out."

"Untie the Harkey groom—we left him near the horses—and he can assist you in finding the surgeon," Devere said.

"Let's get you wrapped so you don't lose any more blood," Rockingham said as he moved quickly to Lord and Lady Churston.

"I'll make sure the Duke and Duchess and their lackeys stay exactly where they are." Devere turned to Monty. "See if you can round up some rope so we can tie up these fellows and the duke."

TWO HOURS LATER, the surgeon had administered laudanum to Charles and stitched up his back. He assured a wailing Georgiana that the wound was not as deep as it seemed, no internal organs had been damaged, and that her husband would have a full recovery. Her tears were now abating, but she continued standing beside her husband's bed—actually the duchess's bed—holding Charles's hand.

Freddie, poor fellow, had been nearly as distraught as Georgiana. "If you apologize one more time," Charles threatened, "I'll be forced to find a new best friend. Remember what the bard said."

Freddie looked puzzled. "'Out, out, damned spot'?"

"No, friend of little brain." Charles eyed his wife.

She turned to Freddie and said, "'All's well that ends well.'"

"Oh, right!" Freddie finally cracked a smile.

Devere managed to get away from guarding their captors and entered the room, a perplexed look on his face. "I don't know if this is good news or bad news."

Georgiana clutched at her heart. "What?"

"The Duke and Duchess of Harkey are dead."

"You killed them?" Charles asked, his eyes rounded.

Devere shook his head. "Harkey asked if I would remove the binding from his wife's mouth. I complied. Then, moments later, he asked if I would permit him a drink of brandy, which I did." He drew a breath. "Unbeknownst to me, he somehow was able to add poison to the glass. He and his wife both drank from the glass."

The room went as silent as a tomb.

Finally, Charles said, "It's best this way."

His wife's gaze met his, and she nodded. "Now, gentlemen, my husband needs his rest."

The others left the two of them alone in the frilly, pale blue chamber.

"Come lay by me, my love," he said.

She climbed onto the tall tester bed, stretched beside him as close as possible, and pressed her cheek to his.

"If it hadn't been for those murders in Manston Stoney, we wouldn't be here today," he murmured. "We wouldn't have married. We wouldn't have fallen in love. Something wonderful came out of grave misfortune."

"That may be, but I know I could never have loved anyone but you. I believe you are my destiny, and somehow, we would have found each other."

His eyelids drifted together, a smile slightly lifting the corners of his mouth as sleep settled over him.

EPILOGUE

Three weeks later

I T WAS ONE of those cold March days when flakes of snow melted as they hit the ground, and no one wanted to be outside. Georgiana was clinging to her husband in front of the fire in their library when Freddie broke into their solitude. He strode up to them and dropped a *Gazette* onto Charles's lap.

"They've finally printed a retraction," Freddie said.

Lord and Lady Churston snapped it up and read the headline on the first page.

Gazette Silent Partner Responsible for Lies, Murder

The long article that took up much of the front page revealed that the Duke of Harkey had put up the money to establish the *Gazette* and sometimes provided articles that the publisher, Hugh Hammond, trusted to be true.

The article went on to say that Hammond had just learned that the late duke and his beautiful duchess had contrived to kill her first husband, a crime to which they confessed before they took their own lives.

Hammond expressed his deepest apologies for printing the late duke's false accusations against the former Georgiana

Beresford, who was now Lady Churston. He explained that Georgiana had known the duchess when she was married to the first husband and that she could destroy the duchess with the truth, causing them to wish to discredit her, hence the lies printed in the *Gazette*.

"Well, my dear wife is finally vindicated," Charles said.

"Vindicated by my darling viscount." She pressed her lips to his.

About the Author

Since her first book was published to acclaim in 1998, Cheryl Bolen has written more than three dozen Regency-set historical romances. Several of her books have won Best Historical awards, and she's a *New York Times* and *USA Today* bestseller as well as an Amazon All Star whose books have been translated into nine languages. She's also been penning articles about Regency England and giving workshops on the era for more than twenty years.

In previous lives, she was a journalist and an English teacher. She's married to a recently retired college professor, and they're the parents of two grown sons, both of whom she says are brilliant and handsome! All four Bolens (and their new daughter-in-law) love to travel to England, and Cheryl loves college football and basketball and adores reading letters and diaries penned by long-dead Englishwomen.

Check out these sites of hers:
subscribe to newsletter – littl.ink/newsletter
blog – blogl.ink/RegencyRamblings
website – www.CherylBolen.com
facebook – fbl.ink/Facebook
Pinterest – littl.ink/Pinterest
Readers' group – facebook.com/groups/2586590498319473

Milton Keynes UK
Ingram Content Group UK Ltd.
UKHW021347280224
438629UK00008B/579